THE DEFIANT

CYNTHIA GILSTRAP

This is a work of fiction. Names, characters, places, and incidents are either the product of the author's imagination or are used fictitiously, and any resemblance to actual persons, living or dead, business establishments, events or locales is entirely coincidental.

I dedicate this first book to Shawn Roberts, the love of my life, who supported me through the whole process and wouldn't let me give up on my dream to be an author. To Katie Wilson, for providing a unique perspective on things and outstanding editing work on my manuscript. To my mom, who always knew I could do it. And to my dad, who is proud of me no matter what I do. Also, a thank you to the folks who keep NaNoWriMo running, you are an inspiration.

Chapters

Chapter 1

Water slapped softly against the rock and was the only sound besides the wet hissing that threatened my peaceful moment with nature. I looked out at the sky, a slate of grey nothing above a catacomb of urban sprawl. The bottle of wine I'd brought to the edge of the little bay was almost gone and I felt as though my burdens temporarily lifted from the nightmare of the past few months so that I could just enjoy the view. Wrapped in a pretty blue afghan I'd scavenged earlier in the day and warmed by a small fire I'd set near the shore, I was enjoying just being alive.

The scrape of rock against rock and the tumble of pebbles pulled me from my trance-like state. I glanced over at the man, rather the remains of a man, who had stumbled on the rocky shore about fifty feet to my left. His grotesque maw worked at nothing, there were black blood stains on the few tattered remains of his shirt and his torn, exposed open wounds were mottled with fetid flesh. He was still too far away to be a problem, but still I touched the handle of my pistol for comfort. Turning my attention, I looked back to the tranquility of my view.

Yeah, he was a zombie. They all were, I guess. I'd been looking for survivors for a couple of months but enthusiasm and hope fades after failing to finding anyone. That hope had been slowly drained away and eroded by time. Despite the number of times I'd joked with guys about not dating them if they were the last man on earth, I couldn't help but feel a bit of desperation for some company.

My brown hair floated around in the breeze and I snuggled into my blanket. The protection spell I'd cast around me would keep them from noticing me or hearing the pop and crackle of my fire. It's handy to have a wizard spell like that to keep people from noticing what is going on under their noses, especially if you needed to cast one of the longer more complicated spells. Unfortunately, I'd had to steal that spell and learn how to use it without the benefit of a mentor or teacher. If the world hadn't turned upside down I might have been worried about being caught using it.

The Elders make the important decision about whether someone is allowed to be trained in the magical arts. That's right, if you have the talent like I do but they don't think you're the right kind of person, then they can deny you the opportunity to learn and punish you if they catch you practicing magic. Without guidance and training most young initiates wouldn't know how to exercise their powers let alone have access to spells and rituals. Magic is sort of like muscle tone, you have to use it or you lose it. The ability to perform spells and magic will atrophy without regular use and training.

There is a testing process they perform on you if they discover that you have magical abilities, the Elders measure your magical potential and make a decision whether to assign you a mentor. A lot of families are specifically watched because magical abilities are a hereditary trait passed down from previous generations. It doesn't even matter if one or both parents have never practiced magic or even know about the magic in their bloodlines, like my family. Of course if neither parent is aware of magical abilities, it gets a little complicated. Still, I've heard that there are ways around that, like winning scholarships to far away schools and the like. I never got that chance. When the Elders made the decision to deny me magical training, I was never told why.

It became my obsession to seek out and collect knowledge and all that was forbidden to me. That someone thought they could tell me what I could or couldn't be or do lit a spark of rebelliousness in me that hadn't faded over the years. I decided to choose my own destiny and that destiny was to become the best wizard ever known. Looking back I realize my youthful arrogance.

It became a game, finding books about real magic before the Elders could store it away without them knowing about me. There's more out there than you'd think. Treasures would pop up in the most unlikely places. I sought out auctions, used book stores, antique shops, libraries and the places you drop off things that are no longer relevant in your life. Occasionally I would score a book or two from these sources because some loved one, unaware of their poor deceased relative's abilities would drop off or sell a box of useless old books. But these were rare and I eventually had to dive into dangerous waters to seek my treasures.

Another sickly hiss turned into a grunt or a groan and the cracking of rocks colliding. I kept my eyes on the rolling water, unwilling to let myself be distracted. I'd eventually have to deal with him when I left, but I was so tired of the violence in this world over past two months that I was willing to stall his demise. I mean really, once I ended him, there would only be another. There would be a world full of others as far as my travels had shown me. Sigh.

The other sources for books became contacts, the contacts became a network and the network got me into illegal dealings. I'd established my network before I'd reached high school, which meant that I had no regard for how close I was to peril. Actually, if I could talk to my younger self, I think she might have admitted to some level of excitement at the prospect of living life on the edge the way anyone might be if they felt immortal and had never truly experienced loss.

Luck was on my side and I let it ride all the way to graduation. It wasn't just the illegal dealings in the mortal world that I was courting disaster, it was the practice of magic at every opportunity I could find. There was more risk in practicing and being caught by the Elders than community service, a criminal record or fines. If I'd been caught I would be considered a rogue. And rogues have a tendency to disappear when discovered under orders of the Elders.

The wind picked up across the bay, the trees along the edge seemed to shimmer with movement and sound masked the sounds of struggle coming from my unwanted visitor. The clouds along the outer edge were tinted with charcoal grey and I knew a storm was on its way. How soon was yet to be determined.

My younger sister Sophie was the only one who got me. Even when I started bringing home books there was no way I couldn't afford on a $5.00 a week allowance, she looked the other way. Sometimes she went as far as distracting our parents while I secured them in my hidey hole. I could tell her my secrets, even practice magic in front of her and she never told a soul. Even when shoplifting turned to break-ins and robberies, which turned into forgeries, she stood by me. I never had to explain myself to her. She just understood.

It was near the time I was about to graduate from high school when I got nabbed in a sting operation with one of the fences I worked with to pay off my debts. I got released on a technicality with the help of a lenient judge but some tough-guy cop wanting to save me from what he thought was a life spiraling into drugs and prostitution, warned me that they were keeping a closer eye on my activities. It was sort of funny to me at the time because my only real concerns at that time were being discovered by the Elders and paper cuts.

My parents helped me seal my arrest record when I turned 18, but they now knew about my interactions with unsavory characters, as they called them. They were nervous, as any parent might be when they are suddenly confronted with the fact that their child's activities aren't all dolls and board games. Of course, they thought I'd fallen into the wrong crowd and could never have foreseen that it had anything to do with magic use. If they'd known that the forgeries of antique books were my handy work and not my being in the wrong place at the wrong time, I would have been in a lot more trouble. Still, I was punished. After that incident, my activities and personal interests were scrutinized so closely that it was hard to even look in a direction without being interrogated.

A breeze, this one a bit cooler than before, whipped around the boulder I was leaning against and my hair flew forward into my face. I tucked the errant strands behind my ears and wrinkled my nose at the smell of decay. He smelled awful. The putrid, sweet smell of death was pervasive and part of the reason why I chose to sit outside in the fresh air. When you're surrounded by that smell day after day, you crave soap and water and all the sanitary conditions that civilization has to offer. I should say, had to offer.

It was Sophie who convinced our parents that my love of books could be more of a career path and an investment in my future. The criminal associations were a childish exploration of myself and part of my rebellious phase, she explained to them. My parents agreed, mostly because it made sense to them based on all those child psychology books that were popular at the time. I don't know that they would have understood my craving for magic and the knowledge that those old books provided. Had they known they would have been a lot less tolerant and possibly sent me away. They're not part of the magic community, nor do they care that it exists. How could they understand what I was so desperately looking for if there was no curiosity or wonder about magic? So, they did what any sane parents would do, they sent me to a shrink for a few years.

It only took a couple of sessions to understand the answers I was supposed to give and the conversations that were healthy to explore. By the end of high school I was diagnosed a normal teenager with a strong interest in books and learning. I began sending out college applications for schools that had a Library Science programs and was accepted by almost all of them. My parents thought that everything was back on track again and settled back into their boring old lives. About a week before this zombie virus broke out my parents had come to see me graduate with a Master's degree. Go figure.

The smell seemed to be getting stronger even with the wind picking up. He was closer now, about ten feet closer. My protection spell worked on undead humans as well as the live ones, but he seemed to be heading on a direct collision course with my impromptu camp. I pulled my pistol out from under the blanket and balanced it on my thigh, gripping the handle lightly. Better ready than sorry. Still, I had a few minutes before he was uncomfortably close and I wouldn't get a view like this again until I made my way to San Fran.

Even though I was in the Bay Area, it would take me a day or possibly two to make it into the city. Traffic was even worse than it was normally with roads filled with abandoned vehicles and wrecks that would never be sorted out. If patterns held up, it would be a traffic jam for miles and miles long. It was frustrating and almost enough to make you cry and give up. Unfortunately that wasn't an option for me.

I shifted so that I could watch the lumbering progress of my zombie companion out of the corner of my eye. For some reason he was determined to get to me and I didn't want to think about the reason why. With one eye on him and one toward the open sky and the bay waters I tried to fight the rising sense of urgency and panic to just enjoy my brief view of beauty. I drained the last of the wine and cuddled into the blanket and let the wind lull me a bit. Just a few more minutes I told myself. There'll be enough time to deal with him later.

I didn't need this. Any of it.

I could have killed him on my way in, problem was I would have brought all available zombies in the area onto the beach. I'm a shoot 'em kind of gal, not a hand-to-hand combat sort. I didn't want to deal with a gaggle of those creatures. Like the horror movies, they seem to track by movement and sound. They have basic sensory functions so it was an advantage to walk softly and kill quickly. If I'd cast the spell with him in it, to block the sound, I stood a good chance of being eaten before I could setup the perimeter of the spell, cast it and sealed the deal. Besides, I needed a break from the killing and the surviving. It's no way to live.

Sophie had no apparent talent or interest in learning magic. She was content to be my assistant, to watch, to play lookout or provide an alibi to our parents when we were growing up. The 'reasonable one' our parents called her. Not sure what that means exactly but it served as a comparison to my description, the 'hellion'. Sophie and I laughed about those nicknames, even up to the end when she…

God, I missed her. I pulled the locket out from under my shirt to look again at what was left of the only person in the world I would consider dying for. She'd come back to our apartment that fateful afternoon, terrified and bleeding and shaking uncontrollably. I pulled every string, every tome, every idea and every stop out to fix her. I remember the smell of dust as I furiously flipped through the older books I'd collected over the years, searching for an answer and finding none. For all the magical lore I'd collected over the years, nothing dealt with the reversal of this infection.

Tears dropped down my cheeks before I could blink them away and I sniffled. I pulled the blanket closer, trying to eke out additional comfort. Damn the wine.

We'd decided that I would bind her in a summoning circle while I worked on a cure to prevent her from doing any damage to me or anyone else. The virus was still just getting started, but enough to cause a panic across the world. All the counter measures and contagion plans fell to the wayside in a matter of weeks, not months or years. Governments, society, all of it crumbled as everyone scrambled to get out of the path of destruction. There wasn't really any time to convene, to determine the best course of action because it hit everywhere all at once and no one could determine the starting point.

Inside the circle she waited patiently, offering the same support she'd given me all my life. She didn't mind the imprisonment but it was a necessity I hated to accommodate let alone admit. It did become my personal window into hell, though.

Watching the infection take her from me, her pain so intense at times I swear I felt it course through me. And I couldn't stop it. I cursed the Elders for denying me the training that could have helped me save her, and at the same time I knew that if they could've stopped the global pandemic they would have by now. But as hard as it was to watch her suffer, it was worse to grant her last wish.

"I don't want to be one of them." A raspy whisper emanated from the crumpled form wrapped in a blanked on the floor in my summoning circle. "I don't want to spread this."

"Don't be such a drama queen." I said, flipping through the book on my lap. I was sitting in the comfy chair in our living room, piles of books stacked around me.

"Listen, I don't—" She spasmed and a wet choking cough erupted from the blankets. "I don't think I have much time left."

"You won't be one of them. I can – let me concentrate so I can fix this." I jumped up to go into the other room.

"Wait. Please." I stopped but couldn't turn around. "Please promise me. Please, before I go. Please."

My throat locked up, hard and painful. My eyes blurred. I couldn't breathe, couldn't speak. I had to find something to stop this.

"Please," she begged. All I could do was nod before hurrying into the other room where I was sure I'd missed something in one of the older books.

I shivered under the blanket. It's worse, you know. Watching something like that. At least when someone dies, they're gone and you know or can pretend to know that they've gone to some peaceful place of rest or something. There is a singular and perverse cruelty in watching someone you love becoming a zombie. Seeing them fight the infection, praying that they'll miraculously pull through. Even when they're gone, I mean clearly gone, you can still see the person they used to be. And all the while you've got this thread of hope, a belief that somehow they can still be who they were before.

Hope is the most painful part of the whole thing. That the cure, whispered like a rumor on the wind, will bring them back to you. That all it takes is holding out until some smarty-pants scientists will find a cure that will change them back from being the monster the virus left behind. You believe for a time that somehow, somewhere they are still in there, in that body. And that presence, that reminder is what keeps that thread of hope alive. I'm sure more than one person joined their loved one waiting for the impossible. I know I almost did.

When I could no longer pretend that she was the Sophie I loved, I... I used some sort of fire spell when the time came. I only vaguely remember the casting. Thinking back I seemed to be moving in a fog, and I remember being so tired it was difficult to move or breathe. I'd lost. I'd lost so huge it was difficult to comprehend. After she was gone, I slept for a while, I'm not sure how long.

When I finally got up and ate it was like I was empty inside. I opened the summoning circle and swept the few ashes that were Sophie into a locket I'd given her when we were kids. Magic fire apparently burns pretty thoroughly for efficient cleanup of 'problems' in the supernatural world. I sealed the locket with magic and I've been moving ever since. It's a reminder to me and an important one.

The clouds were creeping up the sky, looming on the horizon and the wind was coming in quick, cold bursts. It was going to get ugly tonight. There was a faint smell of heather that grows on the banks of the bay, tainted by the overpowering stench of this guy who was still diligently trying to navigate the rocks. His wounds, the decay, they didn't look half as bad as others I'd seen, still the stench was so strong he might as well be sitting next to me…

In that moment I just knew. My pistol was in my hand in an instant and I threw myself forward over the fire in a roll worthy of a kung-fu movie. The blanket was ripped away but still hung by the bony hand-turned-claw of a long decayed zombie slithering over the boulder I'd been using as a backrest. There was no mouth or throat to speak of and I couldn't tell you what gender it was, all I can tell you is that the moment I came up from my roll the gun was flashing and that thing's head exploded into chunks of mottled flesh, congealed blood and bits of bone. The body sagged into the boulder face, the blanket still tangled in its bony grasp. Damn. I was planning to keep that blanket too…

I hadn't taken the time to look at the other side of the boulder, so that was my bad. It may have been trying to get at me since it heard me cast the protection spell. I hadn't found a good way to work in an avoidance clause into the spell, so if the zombies happen to cross the border of my spell by accident or not, they could see and hear me as well as I could see and hear them. Something I needed to work on for the future.

Most of my stuff was in a VW van on the road up topside, so I didn't have to worry about carrying anything out with me. Shaking my head clear of the buzz in my head from the wine, I check to make sure I had enough bullets. I turned to the man who was still trying to slither over the rocks toward me, aimed and fired. The only sound anyone would hear would be the soft rain of gore and the wet plop of his body dropping onto the rocks.

Time to go. Shower, sleep and maybe I'd get lucky and find a survivor tomorrow. A little company would be nice.

Chapter 2

I made my way back to the van without incident. My van was one of those old volkswagon hippie vans I'd scavenged and promptly made a few modifications. I wasn't that great at welding, but I'd managed to melt the edges of some metal plates I'd found over the side and back windows and seal all the doors except the driver side door. I wanted to put a metal piece over the driver side window with an arrow slit, but you'd be surprised how few metal parts there are or how much of a pain it is to learn welding without instruction. Besides I had to keep moving.

The inside of the van was stripped down and utilitarian. There was a curtain I'd taken from a movie theater to separate the front seats from the back of the bus. Behind the front driver's side seat was a little mini kitchenette consisting of a fridge big enough to cool a six pack, a gas stove camp cooker and a box with a flip lid for putting a ten gallon water bottle. I'd long ago abandoned the little sink. Who has time to hook up?

There were a series of plastic office shelves strapped into the door and side next to the kitchenette which served as storage and pantry for food collected along the way. In the back was a bed with my collection of pillows from my travels. And the rest of the area was packed with my arsenal of guns and ammo.

I started her up and the motor rumbled to life. Driving onward I headed through the maze of streets looking for a place to spend the night. Don't get me wrong, the van is great, but there's no shower and I needed to get that freaking zombie juice off me. You can pick the pieces off, but zombie juice drives me nuts until I clean it off.

The homes in San Rafael were all pretty nice looking, small, and likely had all the facilities. The only problem with California homes is they are built for nice weather which means that the windows are bigger and there are plenty of them. I was also noticing how many of them were old and weathered. Easy to break into whether you were looking for sanctuary or fresh, living brains. Most of these wouldn't stop a two-zombie swarm. Whichever one I picked, I'd have to lay some traps and set up a defense tonight.

I picked a pretty yellow home, adobe style siding and clay shingles on top. The driveway was double wide and double long with a carport and an overgrow lawn in front. I backed my van into the drive way as close to the house as I could and waited. Zombies aren't always the quickest things and when a new sound is in an area it's best to see what crawls out of the woodwork before you move around a lot or set camp. I'm not fond of the zombie version of the Psycho movie no matter how badly I needed that shower.

About twenty minutes later a few zombies wandered out into the street. I remained still and just watched to see where they would settle. I call it zombie dusting.

They wandered somewhat randomly, distracting each other with their movements. I'd been playing the scenario of a theory that if chased by a zombie and you ran into a gaggle of zombies and stopped, the resulting movement of the chasing zombie would be taken out by the many. They will attack each other if they get close enough, right? I'd seen it happen before on a smaller scale. It's kind of entertaining in a sad sort of way. They never do enough damage to each other. Yes, these are the thoughts that come to mind when I watch zombie dusting and wait for things to settle.

After thirty minutes and a near fight between two of them, they stumbled off in search of live prey. Looked like they were a few houses off so laying a protection spell on the house and locking it up a bit ought to keep them out. I'd still lay a few traps to alert me if they wandered in though.

I slid into the back of the van and pulled my duffel from under the passenger side seat. Let's see, a sawed off shot gun, a couple of pistols, a pool of wire, some rope, a change of clothes and toiletries. I zipped the duffel shut and put a hand ax on top and grabbed the handles. The seat organizer attached to the front passenger seat had my spell components for the protection spell. I pulled it free and stuffed it into one of the oversized pockets of my jacket.

The area looked clear, but I moved the duffel onto my lap anyway and surveyed the scene. Some movements up the street, but I could see no threats imminent. I slid out of the van and shut the door enough for the latch to click with a whump. I could tell you I was a bad ass, my heart wasn't racing and that my nerves were not on the brink of shattering. I'd be lying. And truthfully, you don't get used to it, not ever.

I assessed the lawn and struggled with the same thing I do every time. Do I go for more coverage or better concealment when casting. I mean, it takes some time and more than a little concentration, but the larger the "safe" area the more room to maneuver. The edge of the lawn near the sidewalk would be pushing things since it might attract unwanted attention. Then again, if I had to fight my way out I'd like a little leeway. I looked both ways down the street. Not much activity here; I would go for more coverage.

There was a hedge between this house and the one next door, so I crossed the lawn at a crouch trying to keep the crunching of walking on the grass as quiet as possible. It gave me three quarters of the front lawn. I placed my duffel on the ground and held the ax in one hand with my spell component pouch in the other. This would do.

I pulled a smooth white stone out and began whispering the words. The faint swirls of golden haze, little fingerlings encased the stone in my palm. I pushed them to the stone and they settled around it and faded. I placed the rock into position and checked the perimeter again.

The other side of the property was a driveway that ended in those tall hedges that spear toward the sky. I approached cautiously, the grains of the ax handle imprinting on my skin, but there was no movement that I could detect. I pulled out another white stone and began to whisper when I sensed something. Movement.

The hedge moved slightly above my head. I looked up, praying and ready to swing my ax to behead anything that come through. A skittering sounded above my head and I could feel the blood draining from my face. Stay still, just so still and maybe it won't…

A flash of grey fur and I jumped back, falling on my ass. The ax landed on my chest, thankfully, instead of clanking to the ground. I scrambled to my feet and looked around to see if I'd drawn attention. My arms and legs trembled and my heart was racing so hard my breath was coming in short gasps. My vision narrowed but now wasn't the time to indulge.

Luckily, I spotted no other movement around. Damn squirrel.

It took me three attempts to get control of my paranoia to cast the spell on my stone, it didn't help that at one point the stone tumbled out of my hand onto the concrete pad. The stone skittered but it did not seem to draw attention. Adrenaline is not your friend when you're trying to concentrate. Remembering the words was becoming rote after months of practice, but the concentration and the focus to direct the magic to do what you wanted is a delicate business, at least for me. Another look around and I glanced toward the double-wide carport next to the house. It was time to check the backyard.

The sun was setting making the shade in the carport ominously dark, but it was the easiest access to the backyard unless I wanted to try scaling a fence. I could see shapes in the back, maybe a fence or something back there. I walked through the carport slowly, ax at the ready. There were plastic tubs, old pieces of wood and some junk stacked in the back between the fence and the neighbor's fence. There was a back door and a gate door with entry into the yard behind the house.

The back door into the house was locked and wouldn't move. It seemed unusually solid, which was good for defense. There were no windows or glass panes on either side of the door, but I assumed it was barricaded. It would save me some time securing it. Zombies don't seem to plan how they get to their intended meals or even have attack strategies; it's up to the survivor to make sure they've covered their bases.

I checked the gate and found it was weathered by sun and time. The hinges held it upright but the wood was bowed and rickety. Splinter city if any pressure was added. The bonus is that it would make a lot of noise if someone tried to make it through here. I peeked through the planks but the low light didn't give me much clue what I was heading into.

A quick glance behind me and I flipped the latch on the gate. The scrape of metal and wood on the concrete was the only sound as I gave the gate a gentle push with the end of the ax. I waited to see if anything was drawn out. No one or thing made its presence known, so I took a quick peek around the corner. In the fading light I could see a yard with trees along the perimeter, a shed on the other side of the gate door, and a cement pad with a picnic table. No sign of life, so to speak.

I pushed the gate a little further open and stepped into the backyard. On the other side of the fence was a stack of old wood and building materials. The wood was weathered and splintery and matched the chipped paint of the old metal shed that looked like rust was working its magic on the walls. A couple of steps in and I could see the shed was locked with a chain and deadbolt. No surprises there, hopefully. The picnic table was like all those at campgrounds everywhere. Those things seem to last forever. The grass was tall, but seemed devoid of weeds, which told me that the yard was lovingly cared for before being abandoned.

I edged around the other side of the shed and found the lawn wrapped around the side of the shed to a couple of trees that had hard green bulbs that would soon be pears. There was a fence across the back of the yard behind the carefully cultivated trees and flower beds. The back fence was in worse shape than the one in the carport. I crept toward it and realized that there was an alley behind this row of houses. Strange. But it might end up being a good route for escape if something went wrong out front.

Kneeling down I cast the spell on the third stone and placed it between the two pear trees. It was close enough to cover the whole backyard. A rumble seemed to build and I looked up at the sky. Dark clouds pressed down and I wondered whether lightning was common in California. Either way, it seemed that the rain was going to be coming down. I needed to hurry.

I moved more quickly when crossing the yard. Haste is not typically a good thing with zombies running around but I hated being wet and I wanted this done before it rained. I picked a spot close to the fence but about the same distance as the other stone from the back fence.

31

The spell cast and the stone placed, I headed back to the carport to cast the last spell. Then I'd cleared the house, without looking over my shoulder to see what sort of attention I'd attracted from the neighborhood.

The carport seemed the best place. It was dark so my movements would be covered, the fence behind me would clatter if anyone tried to sneak up behind me, and I could look out at anyone coming from the front. I put the spell pouch back in my coat pocket and made my way back to the gate door.

Securing the gate behind me I found a place in the center of the carport. It was so dark I slid my foot to find the boxes I'd seen earlier. When I found my spot, I closed my eyes to center myself then opened them to begin the casting. My eyes drifted out onto the driveway, the back of my van, the motorcycle at the end of the drive, the empty street. I reached out with my will to pull the tendrils of the magic on the stones, to stretch and pull them together above the house. I wanted to secure the spell well above the roof.

The familiar ache at my temples and the exhaustion of pushing my will began to weary me. It was almost done. Focus the pain elsewhere. Focus it on the motorcycle, the streetlight highlighting the shiny polished paint job, the metal of the handlebars, the… wait. That wasn't there before.

Just like they can't plan and they can't use strategic advantage when hunting for food, zombies can't drive. This motorcycle was parked, kickstand down and parked in a way that denoted habit and intelligence. There was another survivor. I'd found someone else.

Hope returned with brute force, stunning me. One person was likely. Maybe two if one of them carried supplies in a backpack. It was risky to move around on a motorcycle though, too easy to be pulled off or waylaid when driving through a swarm of zombies. And the sound was enough to bring a horde a-running. I had to know more.

They were parked in front of the house, so perhaps, like me, they were seeking shelter. I had to find them. I moved forward to catch them at the front door and knew that I had forgotten about the plastic tubs as soon as I stumbled. The scraping of plastic and the whoosh of air from my lungs as I tripped would be enough to set me on edge. I had more important things to worry about though. What if they were injured or sick?

With adrenaline as my friend this time, I picked myself up and looked around. My ax! I felt around the area I'd fallen but I couldn't find the thing. Damn. I looked across the driveway but saw nothing. Another quick search of the tubs and I found my ax but it seemed like I'd been searching for too long. My nerves were on edge and panic was starting to take control. Who knew what state they would be in by the time I got done fumbling around in the dark?

I found my way around the carport and had just gotten a glimpse of the front door still shut and intact when I heard it. The sound reverberated off the hills, the houses, and even the windows I stood next to seemed to quake. The sound of a horn blasting in short, screaming calls. It sounded like one of those horns used at football games to cheer your team. And the sound seemed to be getting closer.

The shock of the explosive noise froze me to the spot. I couldn't seem to understand for a moment what was happening. Then thoughts bombarded my brain. They're going to pull everything in a mile radius down on this spot if they don't stop. Were they so desolate that they sought to kill themselves? If I hadn't mistaken the motor for the sound of thunder, would I have been there on time?

The window to my right crashed open as a form flew to the ground and I spun toward it, my axe ready for action. I leapt back and gagged as its head swung toward me. I could see its eyes covered in a cloudy blue film and its face glossy and sticky wet. Ew.

I had a moment to register the number of limbs and it's mobility before it lunged at me. I swung the ax and lopped off the top third of its head. It wasn't an even cut and I was lucky that my ax pulled free, but the blow dropped the thing at my feet, its limbs twitched slightly.

The horn sounded again and this time I moved into action. I had to stop whoever it was before we both got killed. I jogged down the driveway looking for the source of the sound and spotted a man jogging backwards down the street wearing a long dark overcoat with his arm raised up, sounding the blasted thing. Behind him looked like every zombie within a ten block radius following him and more emerging from the surrounding homes. Damn it.

I didn't want to yell, but I had to get his attention, to get him to stop. My heart stopped when he turned in my direction. Even from a distance I could see a muscular build, swift graceful movements and a smile that made me warm inside. I thought I saw him pause, but concluded that he must not have seen me because he sounded the horn again, looked back at the crowd following him and continued walking back toward me. No, that couldn't be. If I wasn't racking my brain with ideas how to save him I'd swear, well, I'd swear he winked at me!

My van only had the driver side door working so our escape would be tempered by how cooperative and coordinated he was. Obviously there were some sanity issues and I couldn't count on his cooperation especially under the circumstances. I mean maybe he'd see that there was another person and give up this foolishness, but it was also a little late to take back what he'd done. We'd have to run for it.

I had enough ammo in my van to take out most of these guys if I only had to spend one bullet per headshot. I couldn't take them all even if they gave me time to find the right ammo for the right gun and allowed me time between reloads. That was also assuming that the noise didn't attract surrounding neighborhoods to increase the number of targets. It's hard to do an impromptu tower defense with just one person. It's easier if you have time and people.

Magic was an option, but I wasn't sure how far I wanted to go down that path. Maybe it was the years of hiding my skills with magic or maybe it was the fear of being exposed. There's nothing like saving someone's life and having them turn around and kill you because they think you're the wicked witch of the west or something. You can never be too careful with who and how you expose those sorts of secrets. People, in general, aren't real forgiving when you break their established reality.

I watched him run, his smile wider and more devilish now as he neared the driveway I was standing on. My heart flip-flopped in my chest and my knees felt like buckling. My head chided my body for its physical weakness, but my heart was hammering too loudly for the rest of me to hear. He seemed to be looking at me now and I thought for a moment that he'd regained his senses. Then he sounded the horn one more time and I cursed his stupidity.

His gaze shifted and I followed the look to zombies making their way up the other side of the street. The dye had been cast and there was nothing to do but clean up the mess. Begrudgingly, I dropped my duffel and pulled out both pistols. He walked past me, tossing the horn to the gutter in front of me and stood in the middle of the street waiting. I watched the little air horn in a can roll a few feet.

I looked up at him for a moment just to understand why. He was handsome, for an idiot. He was a little over six feet tall with dark hair gelled upwards into spikes. Closer now, I could see that he had a goatee and hazel eyes that seemed to shine in delight. In a smooth sweep worthy of a kung-fu movie, he pulled a katana from his back and turned to face the mob.

The newer a zombie, the better speed, mobility and strength they had. Most of these still had their legs and the mobility to move at a light jog. But the dangers of their speed and strength can be amplified by increased numbers and this group had that in abundance. The idiot drove his sword into the first wave of zombies swinging his sword time and time again. His hacking and slashing drove body parts here and there while I stood stunned by the display. The bodies fell and began to stack up. He began to use the hilt of the blade to bash them back but he couldn't cover them all. He was being overwhelmed.

I could barely hear the pop-pop-pop of my gun as I fired shots into the crowd to control the swarm before it overtook him. They kept coming, even the two full clips from my pistols had only given him a few more seconds, almost no more time at all from where I stood. The shotgun was too imprecise and I was less skilled with it anyway. So I did the only thing I could think of to save our skin, I started slinging spells.

The world kicked into slow motion, my eyes assessing the threats and pushing my will into defensive spells, one after another. I pushed and pulled the more aggressive zombies away from vulnerable areas like blind spots and his back. Even as I cast, I knew that neither of us could sustain this for long. Even under the best circumstances a man will get tired. The problem was his actions would take me down with him.

The offensive spells were harder to control and took more energy, concentration and magic to cast, but I tried a few anyway. Between temporary barriers I was able to hold a zombie back for a few seconds, but the more I cast, the weaker I got. The spells didn't last as long, my concentration was becoming more scattered. Then the spells started failing. I couldn't maintain this level of exertion.

My temples throbbed and my gut churned. I was running out of energy to sling and still, they kept coming. More out of survival and necessity, I kept pushing myself. I chanted to myself to keep going, knowing that if I stopped we'd be done and if I didn't I might not make it either.

Suddenly, the man who had called this mess down on our heads turned and ran. My mind shut down. Cold sweat blistering my face with drops, my body shaking with the effort and my limbs unresponsive to my commands, I fell to the ground. And he ran. The zombie horde followed suit, seeming to prefer their targets moving. I watched helplessly as they filed past.

A rumble from the motorcycle engine and I knew. He was going to leave me to die. I lay there trembling, waiting for the end as the motor sounded off down the road. Zombies trailed after him, but it was only a matter of time before they became distracted, before they came for me.

Tunnel vision started in and I could hear ringing in my ears. My breath was getting choppy and the cool breeze was beginning to chill the sweat on my body making me tremble. I heard shuffling and felt a presence beside me. A flower printed dress hem flitted against my arm, the blood dried stiffness scraping at my skin. I tried to lay still, breathe quieter, but I couldn't stop the warm tears building up.

There were no doctors or care centers anymore to take me in and nurse me to health. No ambulances and no spa resorts where you will be taken care of. The real possibility of dying, of becoming one of those things flashed through my mind and suddenly I thought of Sophie. I couldn't just give up. I had to fight. And if I made it out alive, crazy pants on the bike and I were going to have a conversation about what you do and do not do in a world filled with zombies.

The high whine of the engine pushed past the gear ricocheted through the area and the center of focus became him once again. He drove into the zombies, slashing with his katana. Bodies fell and the crowd moved in, tightening the ranks. His tires squealed as he turned for another run. Crazy idiot.

With a renewed determination and not just a little hope that we would be able to pull through this, I pushed myself up on my side and a flash of white hot pain shot through my head. Burn out.

It's one of the worst things about being a wizard. When you push your magic too hard you burn through energy pretty quickly, including the energy that keeps you standing and functioning. The human brain, and wizards are human despite certain propaganda to the contrary, can only handle pushing around magical energies for so long before it has to shut down, to rest. There may be other consequences, but I never had a mentor or resources that explained burn out beyond the basics. Mostly, it feels like a hangover only magnified to epic proportions or maybe a debilitating migraine where every movement and every thought doesn't just hurt, it burns.

I opened my eyes to focus, but I had to work at it. Even the slightest sound felt like a hot poker in my head and the nauseous feeling brought bile to the back of my throat. Most of the zombies were trying to get into the road for a better chance to take him off his bike. There was one zombie though that had its sights set on me. The long hair and hint of a bra gave me a good idea of the gender, because otherwise she was so far rotted it would have been tough to tell her apart from so much rancid meat.

She pulled herself along, inching toward me with single-minded purpose. Normally I'd just kill her and be done with it but I had nothing left. To cast again would kill us both, or worse, just kill me and I'd join the ranks of the undead. My mind couldn't handle that. Wait. The shot gun. I'd forgotten the sawed off shotgun in my duffel.

I looked at my feet to where the bag lay. There was five feet between me and that weapon. The distance, my rolling stomach and the throbbing white pain in my head made me want to cry. All I had to do was maneuver to the bag without crying out and quickly enough not to get snacked on. A spell was out of the question and

41

all that was left was pulling myself along the ground faster than my pursuer.

Moving my foot up a couple of inches, I tried to hook the handle of the bag. Stabbing pain shot up my leg, my muscles clenched and my stomach rolled again. My vision flashed white but since my body was seized with pain I somehow managed to keep myself from gagging aloud. I hadn't quite hooked it. I tried again and thought I was going to die. Miraculously, I managed to loop my foot in the bag the second time.

Glancing up she was still coming for me. I willed my leg to bend, to bring the bag toward me, but the heft of it made my muscles scream. I pulled it a little closer but conceded that I'd have to meet it halfway. My arms felt like cooked spaghetti and they trembled as I reached for the handle. It was too much.

I threw my upper body down as I lunged for the bag before I could calculate the pain involved. I remember reaching wildly for the damn handle and blacking out in the process. I'm not sure how long I was out, probably only a few seconds, but I held the handle of the bag in one hand with no real memory of the pain. The victory was short lived as I looked up to see my adversary, her bony hands within inches of my face. I couldn't pull back, couldn't flinch. My arms were no longer under my control, adrenaline had eked out any strength I may have had to pull the gun and fire it. Weariness of the kind where you have exhausted every muscle beyond its capacity owned my body. All I could do is watch the end come.

I closed my eyes and felt droplets fall on my face and arms. Great, I was going to die in the rain. Hands grabbed at my head and shoulders and turned me face up then released me. At least, I'd get to see Sophie again.

I waited for the pain, the tearing of my flesh and the infection to make its way through my body. I waited. Silence.

Chapter 3

An arm pushed its way under my neck and another lifted my knees and then I was in the air. The smell of leather, spice and something foul tickled my nose but I still couldn't move. The bump of each step jarred me awake even though near unconsciousness followed each time. Suddenly I knew that I was pressed against him, and the crack of wood breaking exploded in my ears.

Stale air, decay and death permeated this place. We spun and I was dropped unceremoniously onto a couch. I could hear footsteps and what sounded like a refrigerator door opening and contents being moved around on the shelves. The fridge closed and various cabinets were opened and the contents shuffled through. Great, I'm dying and he's shopping, I thought.

My mind started to float away, sleep enveloping my senses when my mouth was forced open and a spray of sweet juice poured into my mouth. I coughed weakly as I struggled to swallow the invading liquid before I choked to death. The juice was absorbed almost immediately and I could feel the pull from my body demanding more. When the second spray of juice came my body went into auto-mode, absorbing the energies it needed to recover.

My eyes flitted open and he stood over me with a juice box in one hand and his forefinger and thumb holding my mouth open with the other. When he saw my eyes were open he released my chin, stuck a straw in the juice box and handed it to me.

Hands shaking I could barely hold the thing but my need was so great that I managed to drain the little box. Still weary, still aching all over, but at least I was able to regain basic movements. The body is amazing at recovering on the bare minimum of basic energy sources. A sip of juice and the body starts the timer on just how much you can do to right your situation. I finished the juice box and sank into the couch waiting for the energy molecules to work their way through my limbs. All I wanted to do was sleep. I didn't care about the world anymore, I just needed to rest.

He watched me, studying me as I sat there. I didn't care. When I didn't move and didn't speak, he got up and returned with another juice box. Apparently I was a two juice-box girl. He knelt before me and put the straw into the foil covered hole at the top. I reached for it but he held it out of my reach.

"Who are you?" his voice was deep and serious. I looked at him, then at the drink and shook my head. He rolled his eyes and thrust the drink at me.

"Have it your way. I'm out of here." He stood up and headed toward the door.

"Go ahead," I croaked out and coughed to clear my throat. "Get yourself killed. Be my guest. I'm only sorry I tried to stop you before."

He stopped and flashed a dazzling smile my way, half in and out of the door frame that was broken from our entry. He gave me a once over with his eyes and I glared at him.

"You've got a bit of spirit, babe. I like it, but next time, stick to the guns. Your casting sucks."

He slipped out the door and his boots could be heard clicking down the driveway. I could feel my face getting hot and my thoughts turned murderous. Who the hell was he to tell me... Even my thoughts seemed to sputter. It would occur to me later that somehow he'd known I'd been casting spells. I was a little slow on the uptake at the moment.

I was still too weak to get up, let alone teach the jerk a lesson, so I settled for drinking the rest of the juice box and assessing the damage to the front door. The door frame was splintered but if I cast the protection spell I could barricade the door as needed. I looked at the juice box and decided I might not be able to finish the protection spell tonight. That would be a problem. The other problem was whether the house had accommodations that were reasonable. The smell indicated otherwise.

I pushed myself off the couch and on wobbly legs searched each room of the house. The source of the god-awful smell came from an occupant who'd died in a bed at the back of the house and hadn't been removed. The maggots and flesh melted into the bed and I had to make a run for the toilet. My body wasn't ready to give up the juice I'd just had, so I spent a few minutes dry heaving over the bowl. Maybe the guy who'd dove out the window at me earlier had tried to care for his relative and had become infected instead. I shook my head. Hope, it can be deadly.

The toilet didn't flush and the lid off the back was missing. The shower seemed to have mud splatters, or so I told myself, and as a bonus there was no water pressure. The front door was wide open, I was out of magic for the evening if not for the next week or so. This wasn't the place I wanted to spend the night. Better to take a chance in my van and get a shower tomorrow.

I headed back through the living room toward the front door. Juice box must have been in the fridge. A quick detour to the kitchen and with the last juice box in hand I headed out to my van to begin my tour of the neighborhood. I'd need to find a relatively secure place for the night. I found crazy pants leaning against the door of my van flipping through one of my favorite magazines.

"What the hell do you think you're doing" I charged him, wobbling a little, and stuck my finger to his chest. "You think you can just do something like that and walk away? We could've been killed!"

He raised his eyebrow at the 'we' and then shook his head.

"Don't get your panties all twisted up, babe." He tossed me the magazine that I recognized as one I'd had stashed at the back of my van.

"And what the hell are you doing going into my van," I pushed but with no strength in my arms they just folded until I was leaning into him. I pushed myself up and continued shouting, oblivious to my actions. "What exactly is your damage?"

He remained motionless and silent, watching me. As I stood there I could feel the world spinning and I concentrated on focusing my attention to this idiot who'd almost gotten me killed. The surge of energy, used by my anger, was coming to an end.

"You done?" He said in a quiet voice.

"Not by a long shot," I replied. He smiled and held his position. "Since you didn't seem to hear the question, I'll repeat it. What the hell do you think you're doing?"

"Oh, I'm waiting." He looked over at me then his watch and back at me again. "See, the way I figure it, you've got about five more minutes, give or take, before you crash. Depending on how much of a pain in the ass you are I may or may not decide to leave you here."

My mouth opened and closed but no words came out. I wasn't sure that I wanted to go with him, but if he was right about crashing, which felt genuine, I didn't want to be stuck here. I stepped back to assess my options.

My stones were still spread around the perimeter of the house and I took the time to collect them in silence. He followed and watched silently while the heated debate between my libido, my common sense and my ego raged in my head. When I had my spell pouch together and had collected my duffel I returned to the van.

My head was feeling cloudy but I knew I could at least grab a snack once I was inside the van. My supplies were low but I still had a couple cans of something.

"Get away from my van. I'm done talking to you." My voice sounded tinny to me, but I hoped it was just my ears playing tricks on me.

"What's your name?"

Even at full strength I wouldn't be able to push this guy around, he was too solid. I could try my ax, but in my weakened state I was in no shape to use it. Worse, he might use it against me. There was the sawed off shotgun, but that seemed extreme.

"I'm not moving until you tell me." He threatened. I pulled my thoughts together.

"Casey. Casey Danvers. And you?" I put as much attitude into my voice as I could muster but I could feel myself slipping, weakening. The high from the sugared fruit juice was fading and fading fast.

"Casey, cute name. You can call me JD." He held his hand out and motioned toward the duffel. "We'd best be going if we want to get dinner at a decent hour."

My grip tightened on the handles of the duffel. "What makes you think we are going anywhere together?" I asked. "You're insane. You drew those zombies to you on purpose, you nearly got me killed and now you think to ask me out?"

"I'm not asking." He stood there holding his hand out. He opened the van door and motioned me inside. I hesitated, thinking. "You can either get inside or I can put you in there myself once you pass out."

I had a choice to make. Trust him for now until my strength was recovered or test how serious he was about forcing me into the van and risk being helpless in front of him again. I sighed and threw the duffel bag into the van toward the passenger side seat. I'd play along for now.

I put my chin up and, as dignified as I could, slid into the van's driver side seat. Almost as if he could read my mind about kicking him out of the way and closing the door to escape, he moved to hold the door while standing at such an angle that moving him would be impossible without further maneuvering. The triumphant smile might have been charming but it hinted that he was fully aware of how to control the situation. Thankfully he didn't say anything. I was stuck with him. For now.

I reached over to the passenger side seat to slide over when he grabbed my wrist nearest him and pulled me to his chest. Our faces were inches apart and in my surprise all I could do was look into the yellow-hazel of his eyes. It seemed rather intimate and my instincts screamed to push away but he held me still. Panic welled as I felt him touch my hips and then shifted to indignation and anger as he probed my pockets.

"You could've just asked for the keys, jerk." I growled at him.

"Wouldn't have been as much fun," he said as he tweaked my nose then pushed me back into the van. I kicked back at him weakly and I think I heard him chuckle.

He pushed me further into the van again and I fell over to the front passenger seat. He followed me in, still pushing me over as he climbed into the driver side seat. I grabbed the bar in front of the glove box and pulled myself over and up. By the time I'd righted myself all I wanted to do was sleep. The day was taking its toll on me.

I should have paid attention to where we were going, to the fact that I'd all but been kidnapped by crazy pants and to need to find a safe place to stay tonight. But as soon as the heater in the car came on, exhaustion won me over and I slid effortlessly into sleep.

Chapter 4

I jolted awake when we rolled to a stop. The front of the house looked tastefully landscaped, the steps to the entrance glowed white in the patio lights, and the double doors were elaborately carved with details. This was very high end and my VW bus felt wrong parked in the circular driveway. I looked over at JD to find him watching me, assessing my reaction.

"The house is secure, as is the neighborhood, but I don't expect you'll believe me. You're free to take a look around if you need to." He pulled the key out of the ignition and the silence enveloped us. "I don't advise casting anymore, at least for tonight. I can't stop you, but I suspect you'll do what you like regardless of what I think. You're welcome to come in for dinner and a shower." He opened the van door and jumped out. In the twilight he looked like batman without the mask. I shook my head. I needed to pull myself together.

A quick look around told me he'd tossed my duffel in the back. I looked at it and decided against bringing it in with me. If I didn't like the look of things I'd use it as an excuse to get back to the van and take off. I followed him outside.

He was already unlocking one of the elaborate front doors. I ran to catch up, not wanting to be outside alone after our ordeal, and he waited long enough to hold the door open for me. Our eyes locked and I came into the most spectacular foyer I'd ever seen. A chandelier that looked like it might have real diamonds, an elaborate rug positioned on the floor like a painting you can walk on, a sweeping twin staircase that twisted up to the second floor and pottery with foreign looking plants stretching out of the rims. I was dazzled.

JD pushed me forward. "Make yourself comfortable. Head upstairs. The fourth door to the right is yours." He walked past me and into a sitting room that looked like it belonged to royalty. Then I was alone.

My sneakers squeaked on the hardwood floors as I made my way to the stairs and it seemed that the sound echoed off the walls. I felt like a pauper in my t-shirt, tattered jeans and hi-tops. I made my way up the steps and counted doors as I stepped down the hallway.

This place was so clean it seemed to be a separate world from the one we'd just come from. No stains on the walls or bodies lying around. No smell of decay that I'd come to expect as normal. It was as if the past few months hadn't happened. And of course if I'd become unusually wealthy. I realized, with a twinge of regret, that I'd been staying in all the wrong places.

I found the fourth door on the right and opened it to find more opulence. The bed was huge and canopied in shades of gold and light pink. There was an elaborately decorated dresser next to a vanity station. The handles looked like they were real gold and the mirror looked antique with intricate carvings. I eyed the bed, but there was no way I could just fall into it with how grungy I felt.

There was another door to my left and I opened it to find a marble tiled bathroom with Jacuzzi tub and the biggest towels I'd ever seen. I didn't even know they made towels this big, this fluffy. I touched one to assure myself it wasn't a fur rug or something and pulled my hand back. It was too much.

It took me a few minutes to find the knob to turn the water on and a few more minutes to adjust the water. The steam filled the room and I could feel the knots in my back releasing, my muscles relaxing. I peeled my clothes off and slipped into the Jacuzzi tub. The water bubbled around me and the jets worked against my back.

Just like in the car my mind wandered and I fell into a half wakeful state. Thoughts floated through my head randomly and I was blissfully unaware of the world around me. I let myself relax for the first time in months.

I looked out over the bay, the grey of the water and the grey of the sky subtle shades different from each other. The whole world was shades

*of grey. The rocky shore was empty and the
quiet was comfortable. She stood close to the
water, her jeans a vivid blue and her favorite
red sweater was so bright it was hard to look
at. She turned and smiled at me.*

"Casey, come look." She waved me over.

*"Sophie, I'm sorry." Even though I was
whispering I knew she could hear me. She
shook her head and laughed that familiar laugh
that I'd heard all our lives.*

*"Silly, it's not your fault." I looked away.
"Don't be like that. Come look."*

*I pushed myself off the rocks and made my way
to where she was standing. She turned to look
at me then pointed out over the water. I looked
at her, standing there, more alive than I'd ever
really seen her. There should have been some
way to save her, to...*

"Look, Casey, just look."

*"There's nothing out there for me, Soph. I can't
do this all by myself." I felt her eyes on me.*

*"You won't be alone, Hard Case," she smiled
at the nickname she'd given me when she was
in high school. "You will find your way, the one
you always knew was out there for you. And you
won't be alone."*

*The warmth, the kindness emanating from her
was nearly palpable. She pointed again to the
water and focused out into the far reaches of*

the bay. I turned to see what she'd been pointing at.

The water seemed to spin and spiral downward around the middle of the bay. It was difficult to see from the position we were in, but the waters turned quickly, violently. There was no wind, nothing to indicate where this anomaly had come from.

"What is that?" I asked, moving closer to her to get a better look.

"That's what you have to stop, Casey. You have to unspin it or the whole world will be sucked down into it."

Suddenly I was under the water, but I wasn't holding my breath or feeling that enclosed pressure being under water provides. I could see the water spinning, but it could just have easily been a tornado. Floating closer I came to see the spikes and froth that appeared to be water were actually the hands, limbs and heads of people. The closer I got the more detail I could see. Not just people, zombies.

"What am I supposed to do, Sophie." I was frustrated. I'd tried everything I could think of, didn't she know that? If I couldn't stop it from happening to her, how could I "unspin" this monstrosity?

No answer. I looked around me, but she was gone. Still I kept floating closer, unable to stop

*myself. No, I thought, no I don't want to go in
there.*

*I heard her voice in my head, "You have to
unspin it or we'll both be lost."*

*Struggling didn't seem to do any good. I kicked
and tried to wave my arms to alter course or
change directions. Nothing was working. I
could see the angry maws working, the decayed
hands reaching out for me, the eyeless sockets
and the weeping gashes of the zombies. I had to
find a spell, I had to find something.*

*I searched my memory for something that
would help as I was swept closer to the
spinning, frothing doom. Every spell I cast
failed to go off and none of it helped alter my
path. The hands grabbed at me, they tore at my
clothes. The glaze-eyed visage of my sister
before I'd granted her final wish appeared in
the storm. She lunged to bite.*

The water sloshed over the side of the Jacuzzi
tub as I tried to bolt into a standing position and
slipped, hitting the side and bottom of the tub.
My breath came in quick gasps and my chest
hurt from the tension. I gripped the sides of the
tub as reality filtered back in and I let the
polished room bring me back from the
nightmare. Suddenly I didn't want to be in the
water anymore.

Chapter 5

I toweled off and returned to the bedroom. My clothes had vanished and on the bed lay a pair of women's trousers and a pretty pink blouse. It looked like the kind of thing I'd wear to an interview or to do office work. I touched the fabric and it felt silky and expensive. Probably he was just washing my clothes, I told myself, they were a bit dingy after rolling around with zombies this afternoon. Still, the clothes he'd chosen seemed a bit too formal for a casual evening hiding from the undead.

After searching through the available clothes in dresser drawers I discovered that most of the clothes were around my size. I found a pair of matching bra and panties and offered a silent apology to the woman whose clothes I was raiding and put them on. Finding nothing less extravagant, I decided the trousers and blouse were acceptable. The trousers were a little long, reaching to the floor, but the blouse fit perfectly.

As I was checking myself in the vanity mirror I heard movement. JD was standing in the doorway; he'd changed into a dark t-shirt and black slacks. He'd shaved the five o'clock shadow making his goatee look polished and his hair looked damp as if he'd bathed too.

"Where'd you find this place?" I asked. "I mean, you have the key and all."

He stepped into the room. "It's sort of a family estate in the area."

"Family…" I paused to consider the implications then let it drop. My memories were still a bit raw, obviously, and there was no telling how fast anyone else would recover from their own flavor of loss.

"This is, or was, my sister's room. She had it decorated to her specifications." He looked around the room and his gaze settled on me. "You look better in those clothes than her, though."

I could feel myself blush as I looked at him, then looked at my reflection in the mirror. My hair was just past my shoulders, dark and would be incredibly tangled if I didn't get a brush through it soon. I'd never needed mascara or eyeliner, my lashes were naturally dark and outlined my blue eyes without needing help. My skin was pale, but it'd been a while since I'd been able to be carefree enough to tan. But he was right about the clothes; they looked great.

"You need heels with those pants," he said casually. "But don't feel like you need to pick a pair out unless you feel like it."

I smiled at him and walked over to take his arm. I'd seen movies, you know? Besides, what's the harm in living a little bit of the movies now and again? His eyebrows rose a millimeter but he escorted me down the hall, down the stairs and into one of those dining rooms that you see in the magazines with the perfect homes. Only the table was set for two and there were steaks already plated and steaming.

"Steak and potatoes, huh?" The corners of his mouth twitched upward.

"Don't tell me you're a vegetarian. That doesn't bode well for our continued association."

I laughed. It was a real laugh, something I could hardly remember doing since the outbreak. I took my place at the table, letting him pull the chair out for me before taking his own spot.

My mouth was watering at the aromas rising from our food. It had been a long time since I'd had anything that wasn't canned and steak was almost unheard of nowadays. The steaks were grilled perfectly and it was all I could do to keep from ripping into it. I looked up at JD, unsure of what the protocol ought to be, and saw him pulling the steak knife and fork from the placemat.

We ate in silence. The steaks were soft like butter that melted in my mouth. I tried to savor each bite as it may be the last time I had fresh meat and this was as good as any I'd had in my life. After living on canned rations this was heaven, but I couldn't help but wonder how he'd come to have steak. The grocery stores were all in shambles and overrun and I hadn't seen a cow in all my travels. I suppose, though, if the electricity were maintained that a freezer could keep fresh some supplies.

"I figure we can get my bike tomorrow morning. We'll just stay here tonight, if that's ok with you." I looked up to see him watching me again. "You can sleep in my sister's room. We'll be safe here. I've already taken the liberty of clearing the area."

"Is that what you call it?" Even as I realized it was pointless to be angry about it, I couldn't help my temper from flaring. "Nearly getting yourself killed. Nearly getting me killed."

"I don't recall asking you for help." He said between bites. "In fact, I was holding my own out there. Try to think back and remember who needed saving."

My blood began to boil at all the things I wanted to say to such an absurd assessment. The arrogance of the man was hardly bearable. Who was he to… How was I… Damn. My thoughts were sputtering too.

"You know," I said after a few minutes of getting control of myself, straining my voice a little trying to keep my voice level. "There are better ways to handle your fru—"

"Don't," he shook his head. "I don't need any pop-psychology crap, any advice or any suggestions. These are fucking zombies. There is no other purpose for them than to feed on us and each other. If I wipe a few out along the way, well, hey, I've at least made a difference. But don't sit there and think you know me. You don't."

My eyes dropped to my plate as I thought about how little I actually knew about the man sitting across the table from me. I couldn't know what he'd gone through. Maybe it had been worse than what I went through. Also, after his offer of shelter and helping me out of a tight spot, I wasn't being the most respectful of guests. The scrape of metal on dishes told me that he'd resumed eating. I couldn't think of any other way to repair the damage, so dinner continued in silence.

When we were done he belched and turned to me with a smile, apparently previous conversations forgotten. He stood up, pushed his chair into place and carried his dishes through a swinging double door, presumably the kitchen. I followed.

I'd seen restaurants smaller than this. I gaped at the open space, the counters, including the island and all the amenities of a professional kitchen. The cabinets were understated but you could tell they were of quality design and manufacture, the marble counters gleamed under the lights and the floor space was big enough to allow five or seven people to work without coming within five feet of each other.

JD motioned for me to bring my dishes to him. To my surprise he rinsed the dishes and put them into a dishwasher near the sink. When he was done he poured soap into it and turned it on.

"TV is a little sketchy; I tried this morning when I got in. They need someone to work the tapes at the stations because it's all static. I might have a couple of movies if you're interested?"

I shook my head. It was too surreal, like we were teenagers on a sleep over or a date night with his parents out of town. Everything since we'd got here was quiet and peaceful and though it was tempting to let the fantasy continue, we needed to be a bit more practical.

"I've got board games around here too if you're not into the movies." He took off before I could tell him I was too exhausted to stay up much longer. I trailed after him, but the few seconds it took me to catch the door and follow him, I'd lost him.

The room I was standing in was smaller with a floor-to-ceiling window pane and long artfully draped curtains to either side, secured twice down the twenty foot length. Night had fallen and it was pitch black in contrast to the softly lit room. The thought of someone watching or throwing themselves against the window kicked my paranoia into gear and I could feel myself tense up in reaction. Was this place really secured?

"Over here," JD appeared in a doorway to my left, hidden between two bookshelves. I followed him through the doorway, down a hallway and into a room with furniture that looked like it belonged in a fancy lawyer's office. The coffee table had been cleared and a stack of games were piled to one side.

"You pick." He offered with a sweep of his hand over the stack of board games. I looked at the games, but couldn't get enthused about any of them.

"I'm really tired." I shrugged. A flicker of disappointment and it dawned on me that as lonely as I had been for company, I might be the first company that he'd had since civilization had rebooted. What would one game hurt?

I tried to think of something quick, something that wouldn't take a lot of time to setup, clean up or play and could be halted at any time. Before I even knew what I was going to do I blurted out "How about Truth or Dare?" He gave me an evil smile and I immediately regretted my choice.

"You're braver than you look." He took a seat on the couch while I chose one of the chairs. "Guests go first."

I looked around the room looking for something safe to focus on. He seemed to notice my attentions and answered my unasked question.

"This is my family's summer home. My father uses the place for business dealings when he needs to be in town and my sister drops by occasionally to do—well, whatever it is she does." He shifted in his chair a bit. "So, are you going to start or shall we sit here all night looking at each other? No preference, mind you."

I sighed. "Fine. Truth or Dare?"

He chose truth and my mind raced. What do you ask a total stranger who obviously has a bit of a death wish? Still, this was an opportunity to get to know him a little better. Maybe this would work out better than I'd hoped. Suddenly I knew what I wanted to ask.

"Where were you when you first knew the zombies were actually walking the earth?" He looked at the ceiling as if thinking about it.

"I was driving the back roads from a cabin I'd rented out on a lake when I noticed some guy limping across the road. I hit the brakes just missing him. He didn't even move." He paused, seeming to lose himself in the memory. "I was reaching for the door to see if there was anything I could do for him, but before I could get out he turned toward me and jumped on the hood of my car. I was outraged of course, until I saw that his eye was dangling out of its socket."

His voice got distant as he recalled it. "I started to notice other things as I watched him. He had bite marks on his face and arms and he was covered in congealed blood that smeared like mud on my windshield in streaks. He kept throwing himself on the hood and sliding back down and then trying again and again as if he couldn't figure out what the door was for." JD seemed to shake himself back from the memory. "I wondered what he was on. I should have yelled or gotten out and pulled him down and tried to offer medical assistance, but I was too shocked, you know? I mean, here was some nut all bloodied up and attacking me through the front windshield of my car. I didn't even see the other one until I saw arms reaching in the passenger side window."

"She, I don't know where she came from, but this woman had come around the side of the car and reached in through the open passenger window. Scared the hell out of me." He smiled and looked at me, seeming to ask my pardon. I didn't want to interrupt, but I could tell him that my passenger side door was sealed shut for a reason.

"I know it sounds bad, but I hit reverse and dragged her half mile before she fell out. The smell was God awful, like, well you know." He got up and walked to a cabinet and pulled out a bottle. He poured an eighth of a glass for each of us and returned with the drinks. "I ran over her. Backed over her twice then drove off. I was a bit crazed at that point and I guess I didn't actually know that they were zombies, but I knew something wasn't right. Amazing thing is at the time I thought it was a trick of the light or something when I saw her get up again in my rearview mirror."

"It took about fifteen minutes to drive to the next town and there I got a better understanding of the situation." He spun the amber liquid in the glass then sipped at it. "I'd been at a cabin on leave from school. The pressure was getting to me and I needed a break to get away from it all. Too far away from it all, I guess."

I nodded reflectively and took a sip. My throat shut down except for the coughing fit. JD chuckled but didn't do anything to assist. He drank his glassful.

"Some people can't handle the good stuff." I barely heard him through my barking coughs. My throat was raw from the alcohol and clearing my airways. "My turn. Truth or dare?"

"Truth," I croaked although I was in no condition to talk. Still, fair was fair.

"You're a wizard. Why haven't I heard your name before now?"

If I hadn't choked on the drink I might certainly have reacted more to such a direct question. Maybe it was the secrecy I shrouded myself in when it came to that aspect of my life or maybe having it said out loud still made me nervous despite the lack of other wizards to provide consequences.

"I'm a private person." My voice was rough and I had to wipe the tears from my eyes. "I don't advertise."

He laughed. "There's no shame in still being an apprentice at… How old are you?"

I threw a pillow at him and he laughed harder. It was a deep throated laugh and despite my annoyance, it was nice to hear.

"Maybe it is a little embarrassing, I mean really, only a novice would cast to burnout without having a contingency plan." His eyes searched mine. "Who's your master?"

I took a swig and smiled. "You're out of turn. Truth or dare?"

"I'd choose a dare, but I'm not sure it would be much of one. You seem pretty mild mannered for a wizard." I let that one slide. He didn't know how wild I could be and I didn't see any need to educate the fool. "Let's try, Truth." He didn't look all that terribly worried. In fact, he relaxed further into the couch kicking his boots up on the coffee table as he waited for me to come up with something challenging.

I looked around the room, trying to think of something clever. I spotted what looked like a family portrait on the far wall. Wait, family might be a poor choice of topics. No need to drudge up bad memories, let alone spot light my own personal tragedy.

"Have you found any other survivors?"

"I've looked." He looked at me, sitting perfectly still as if trying to read me. "Still looking in fact. Couple of friends here and there that I thought might have weathered the storm. I'm heading into San Fran tomorrow to have a look around."

I raised an eyebrow but waited until I was sure he was done speaking. "So you're looking for friends and not family? Were they, I mean if it's bad you don't have to, but…" My voice trailed off, but my inner voice screamed in embarrassment over my blunder.

"My family is incommunicado somewhere in Europe. When the lines went down and the satellites stopped syncing I lost the ability to get in touch with them. Unless I can find a pilot or stock a boat for a long voyage overseas I won't know what happened to them. That's not really reasonable for a variety of reasons, least of which is lack of skill. I won't pretend to know whether they are still alive somewhere, but it doesn't help to think about it if there isn't a way to know for sure." He stood up and walked to the liquor cabinet for another drink. "Not sure I want to see them if they've been turned into one of those things anyway, you know?"

I nodded and took another sip before I remembered. I coughed again, breaking the silence. Out of the corner of my eye I saw him smile and shake his head then down his second drink. He walked over, grabbed my glass and poured another one for both of us.

"You'll get used to it." I looked at him through bleary eyes. "But, you have asked two questions so that opens the door for a double on the next 'truth or dare' challenge."

I stood up and stretched my legs. "You know, I think I'm going to get some sleep. It's been a long day." I started walking toward the door we'd come in. It was the best way to find my way back without getting lost. At the door jamb I was turned roughly and pushed against the frame.

"Can't just leave a game of 'truth or dare' without answering when it's your turn." With his body pressed against mine all I could feel was solid muscle and his breath smelled like bourbon. He pressed the drink into my hand and pulled me back into the room by my other hand. "Truth or dare."

"Fine. I'll take a truth and a dare, then we're even and I'm headed to bed." He looked smug but I pretended I couldn't see it.

"Let's see. What do I know about you." He looked up at the ceiling, mocking deep thought. "You are a private person, you don't plan contingencies for burnout and can't handle good bourbon. What should I ask…"

My head felt full, still recovering from the burn out and I could feel myself fighting against the exhaustion that was wearing me down. Maybe it was really time for bed.

Chapter 6

I woke with the sun streaming in through the window filtering through the canopy drapes that flowed around the bed. I lifted my head but put it back onto the pillow as gently as I could to reduce the pounding sensation. Cold sweat beaded across my forehead and upper lip and my stomach tightened. Even thinking hurt.

The bathroom was across the room and with the complication of the canopy drapes I might make it to the toilet before throwing up. Lowering the curtains was another matter. What had I been thinking getting drunk like that? Even as I posed the question I knew. I'd been alone too long, afraid too long, running too long. Now and again you just need the night off.

I slid carefully to the edge of the bed, trying to find the edge of the covers by pulling up the blankets that hung over the side onto the bed. My hand was free when I felt the bed shift and an arm wrapped around my naked body pulling me closer to its owner. Wait. Naked?

Panic jolted through me which began the cascading events that I knew would end up being a mess. I tossed JD's arm back behind me, scooted to the end of the bed, waved my arms wildly to get the canopy out of my way and half stumbled/sprinted to the bathroom. I made it to the toilet before I was sick.

Between heaving all my insides, flushing and shaking in a full body sweat from the migraine I asked myself what I'd done last night. Oh god, what had I done? Round and round for what seemed like forever until I was so wrecked, so empty and so weak I couldn't have cared less what happened next. A zombie could come in and I would welcome the end. Well, maybe not welcome but I'd be hard pressed to concentrate on any of my spells and being naked. And, being naked I was without a gun anyway.

"You almost done in there?" With bleary and I'm sure bloodshot eyes, I tried to glare at him. I think it might have become a squint in the additional light he'd let in by holding the door open. He walked in and I turned my head from his nakedness. The sound of running water assaulted my ears and I groaned as I felt another dry heave coming.

He knelt beside me, wiping my face with a cool damp towel. It felt like a caress and it shamed me to think I'd sunk so low, that I'd become this pathetic. I knew better. Tears welled up in my eyes and I sniffled.

He stood and walked back into the bedroom. Probably giving me space to cry my eyes out in private. It was so considerate, damn him. I felt the room darken and realized he'd closed the bedroom curtains and heard the footsteps swish back to the bathroom.

I braced myself, trying to pull all the dignity I had left. "I'll be ok, just a little hung over. Just give me a few minutes and I'll be fine." My voice didn't feel as throat wrenching as it felt and I only winced a couple of times. I waited for him to leave.

JD walked to the shower instead and started the water running. I admired his form, while he wasn't looking. For a fleeting moment I thought I hadn't done half bad before I squashed that line of thought. It was a one night thing, I told myself. We were just seeking comfort in each other.

He stepped closer bent down and lifted me in the air. My stomach rolled at the motion but I held it in check. He walked toward the shower and set my feet onto the tile while supporting my body until he was sure I could stand on my own. The water tickled my toes with cool droplets. My head was dizzy and I turned to tell him that I wasn't up for this when he wrapped his arm around my waist and pulled us both under the stream of water.

I gasped at the sudden emersion into cold water. "Hold on, it'll feel better in a minute." I couldn't speak and his hold was iron-tight even with my weak struggles. We stood there with me sputtering obscenities under my breath and water running down our bodies. When I finally let myself sink into the inevitability of being held under the shower, my head began to clear.

The shower was… well, let's just say it was strange to be in a shower and the focus outside of a show-me-yours-and-I'll-show-you-mine game was to get clean and for some reason stay very, very cold. Maybe it was for the best. It did seem to help a bit and when we were done we both dressed quietly and without making eye contact.

He finished before I did and left the room, leaving me to wonder who this guy was and whether I could puzzle out the dichotomy between last night and the zombie-slaying maniac I'd nearly died trying to save. I took my time getting ready, knowing I might not get this sort of quality restfulness in the days or weeks to come. By the time I was ready to head out and search for JD my stomach was rumbling.

The house was even more beautiful in the light of day and I searched for JD wondering at all the art and rooms I passed. I caught up to him as he was plating breakfast. We enjoyed biscuits and sausages with coffee. I avoided the frozen orange juice as it just upset my stomach, but JD picked up my slack and finished it off. When we were done both of us worked at cleaning up the kitchen then headed to the foyer where we stood for a few minutes.

"So we need to get your bike." I looked at JD and he stared back. I squirmed inside. If we hadn't slept together this would have been a lot easier, I thought. He made no move toward the door, no comment.

"Look, can I get my keys, please?" He smiled and walked toward the door.

"I think we'll need supplies if we're going into San Francisco. My sister's clothes just don't look right on you." He stared walking toward the door. "You've got a good selection of equipment in your van, but we need to condense it to something a little more portable."

"Wait a minute. San Fran?" My voice squeaked.

"Yeah, I'm looking for a friend of mine and you think you have a line on someone who you were certain would still be around, remember? We discussed this last night." My mind raced through the few memories I'd had of last night. Dinner, truth or dare, drinks and what else? Crap.

"I've got clothes in the van I can switch to and my van is specially adapted for driving around." I tried to sound confident as though last night wasn't a complete blank and I followed him outside into the cool morning air. "The doors are sealed except for the driver side and there are living supplies that can be used in a pinch."

"Listen Casey, here's your reality check. Those doors being sealed could just as easily been sealed by locking them. Zombies don't work door handles. The window coverings while they

77

seem like they are solid aren't as tightly welded as you think they are. Enough pressure and they're no more useful than a window. It's not really passenger friendly and there are no options if you get trapped inside." JD continued to walk around my van and point out additional weaknesses of my vehicle and its defenses.

The gas mileage was atrocious; the van was rusted in places indicating it hadn't been taken care of in its long, long life, the acceleration was abysmal and the off-road functions that may be necessary for rolling over zombies in a pinch was next to none.

The more I listened the less I could find fault with his assessment. It only seemed safe, but could very easily become a death trap. The moment it broke down or I got into trouble, I could see where I might find myself unable to get out or defend myself. I sighed and as if on cue, he wrenched open the driver side door and jumped into the back. I heard the rattle of guns and canned food goods and just waited for the rest of it.

"We can take the guns, but most of this crap has to go. We can dump it when we grab my bike." He jumped out and motioned me into the van.

"Hold on, cowboy," I said shaking my head. "Sure this rust bucket may not be as safe as some vehicles, but a motorcycle is more of a death trap than my ride. There is nothing stopping those things from pulling you off and they are harder to take difficult terrain when there are two people on the bike. And what's this 'we' deal anyway? I thought you were a lone wolf or something." He strolled over to me, put his hand to my lower back and pushed toward the van.

I stumbled forward and turned to give him a dirty look. He winked and then nudged me again. Men.

"Women, always wanting to shop." When I turned to hit him, he grabbed me around the waist and tossed me backward into the van. My ass landed on the driver seat and my head hit the passenger seat. I pushed myself up and angled to kick him, but he grabbed my ankles and pushed them down to the floor and scooted into the driver seat.

"Men, always pretending that they don't enjoy it too." He guffawed and started the van.

It took over an hour of arguing before JD conceded that his motorcycle was not really a much better choice than the van. He thought he'd made a damn good argument for speed, agility and the ease of fueling and repair. My argument that should we find other survivors and how to carry the gear we would need was equally compelling. In the end I think he agreed just to shut me up.

A few hours after canvassing neighborhoods we happened on a hot pink H1. This Hummer was a massive beast of a vehicle except for one thing. The garish color contrasting with the deathly grey and lifeless neighborhood made it hard not to see. I jumped up and down in my seat as I pointed to it.

"It's perfect. JD, stop. That ought to do, right?" He looked at the vehicle with such disdain that I was afraid he might blow it up. "Don't tell me you don't like Hummers."

"It's not that. I just don't want to be seen in the Barbie doll version of a perfectly respectable vehicle." He shook his head then yelled shaking his fist in the direction of said Barbie-mobile, "Why would anybody in their right mind do something like that!"

Though I hated the color too, I wouldn't admit to it and I just couldn't help giggling at his reaction. The thing was pretty awful, but it had the advantage of being big, hard to flip, easy to secure and hard to stop. Aesthetics aside, it was a good vehicle. He started to pull away but I grabbed the keys and turned the ignition off.

"Let's check it out." He made a face and kept his eyes to the steering wheel. "Come on. It's the best one we've seen yet."

"Hey, you know I think I remember a dealership around here. Ford. We could get one of those Expeditions. Brand new, you'd like it." I shook my head.

"H1, dude. Think about it. Close as we can get to a military vehicle. Besides, no one but zombies will know and they don't talk." I gave him an overly cheerful smile and pushed him against the door. He groaned and jumped out, turning and offering me his hand, which I took.

I reached back into the van and pulled two pistols out. I offered one to JD but he shook his head. There was broken debris on the ground and he picked a limb out of the mess. We approached slowly, cautiously.

The H1 was parked curbside but the front door was ajar. There was no activity on the street but we still moved quietly. If this was a viable deal we'd need some time to load the rest of the weapons into the back before taking off.

JD motioned to me that he was going around the side and to cover the path between the van and the Hummer. I knelt down and surveyed the area in slow circles, trying to cover every angle that might be a direction for attack. By the second rotation, JD had made his way around the vehicle and was sneaking up on the driver side door.

This thing looked huge compared to my van, the previous owner had to have raised the vehicle up. The tires were almost as big as I was. JD reached up for the door handle then threw the door open and swung in front of it, the branch ready to swing at anything that would leap out. Nothing.

He gave me a look then hefted himself up and into the cab, looking in the back for any remnants of the previous owner, alive or otherwise. He looked back and gave me a thumb up sign. All clear.

While I was sorting through my possessions inside the VW, JD managed to scavenge a large green duffle to fit all the guns and ammo piles we'd decided to take with us on the trip. He rolled his eyes at the piles of clothes and pillows.

"Seriously, woman." He knocked a pile of pillows over. "We're headed to the mall next. Pick up some clothes and then head toward San Fran. You don't need all this stuff."

In the end we left with the basics. The guns and ammo were stored in the back with a few choice pieces in the front for easy access. Some gardening tools and baseball bats, which I thought was excessive since I couldn't take all my stuff. But, I suppose you can't kill a zombie with a pillow collection, unless you were really creative about it.

We drove for miles, dodging abandoned cars, debris, the left over destruction of a civilization gone wrong. The mall was a mess with packs of zombies in the parking lot. It would have been a lot of work to get in and out and in the end we decided that maybe the boutique stores would be a better option. People don't think, zombies - let's go to the boutiques! They head for a place where there are supplies or places where they've been before. So, ultimately we decided that the shopping in San Fran might be a bit better.

"So, how do you know this friend?" I asked. He kept his eye to the road and didn't answer. I was afraid that perhaps we'd covered this information already. Maybe it was a girlfriend or something. We travelled for a while in silence until we came to the last bridge.

The cars were packed onto the bridge, all rows had cars facing toward us. Everyone had been trying to flee the city. Accidents had held things up, infected suddenly losing their humanity, and then no one was safe. Unfortunately there wasn't any room for the H1 to fit, even if we played Tetris with the cars.

I looked at JD, but he was looking out the window at something on the road.

"Want to go on a little bike ride?"

Chapter 7

"You're insane," I whispered furiously at JD. He continued to park the Hummer on the outskirts of traffic near the toll booth.

"It'll be fine, don't get your panties in a twist." He pulled the e-brake and grabbed a rifle from between the seats. "I've ridden a bike for weeks now and I haven't run into anything I couldn't handle. Besides, look at that mess. How do you think we're going to get into San Fran? Fly?"

He was out of the car before I finished rolling my eyes. I jumped out and fairly stomped over to him where he was trying to retro fit a backpack into weapon locker. I reached up to the back door of the H1.

"Let me rephrase," I said in the calmest voice I could manage. "You're insane if you think we can make it into a city with a dense population of zombies, no doors or windows to protect us and the only fall back plan is our weapons which will run out pretty damn fast. All it takes is one swarm, their attention on the sound of that motorcycle, and we're dead."

"You're a glass is half empty kind of person, aren't you?" I stood there waiting for him to finish but he just continued to pick through the weapons and tools, selecting items and putting them in the backpack. When he finally turned, he held the backpack out as if to help me on with it. I motioned impatiently for him to continue.

With a sigh, "That bridge is packed with cars and debris. The Hummer won't fit and if you look more closely, you'd be hard pressed to find any vehicle that could fit as well as the motorcycle. That baby there will not only get us across without having to walk and fight our way across the bridge, but will also keep us from having to camp there, without supplies I might add, when it gets dark. The cycle will get us there fast and we can skip over the nasty bits if we want.

"Now, if we get across that bridge and find the streets packed with busted cars and debris, we can use the cycle to move around, faster than they or we can run. But, if we find the streets clear and a wall of zombies, then we will grab a car if it'll make you feel better. Just don't fool yourself into thinking that being in a car is any safer."

He walked around behind me as he continued. "An enclosed area, like a car or a house may seem like a layer of protection, but can be turned into a trap under the wrong circumstances. Windows break, metal bends, wood breaks. The only thing that keeps you away from them is speed and distance."

I stood my ground. "So why are we even doing this then?"

He grabbed one of my arms, then the other and stuffed them through the straps and slid it up to my shoulders. "Densely populated areas increase the odds of finding survivors, babe. Besides, you have a better plan?"

I bit my lip. He had a point about mobility and there would be more places to stock up on supplies in the city. Still, my survival instincts screamed that this was the worst idea, the worst course of action. There were other wizards and other houses I could raid for the books I needed.

Gschuck was a name that I'd found mentioned in a couple of the more advanced books on magic and in one tome I'd found an address in San Francisco for the guy. Gschuck'd come up with some pretty tough spells and I hoped he was a heavy hitter in this situation, at least enough to be alive to ask some pertinent questions. I had some far-fetched hope that he could set to rights my little sister's untimely demise, maybe even with my help. I knew that was far-fetched too, but I needed to believe that something could be done. Besides, now that I had a companion, although he was crazy, I suddenly had an attack of self-preservation.

I pushed down the panic and tightened the straps until the backpack was snug against my back. If we were going to do this, we'd better get it over with. Hope, it's a cruel mistress.

"If I die, I'm going to be really pissed at you." I stalked toward the bike and pretended not to hear the soft laughter coming from behind me. He closed up the H1 and locked the doors. Maybe we'd see it again. If so, it'd be secured.

It took twenty minutes of fiddling to get the bike started. My worried and unconvinced glances rolled off JD's back like water. When he got the thing started and the motor erupted into an explosion of sound in an otherwise silent world, I tensed. I was ready for zombies to roll out of the cars en mass to kill us, but nothing happened, no movement.

JD reached for me and I jumped onto the back. After adjusting an uzi that was strapped across his back, I was able to wrap my arms around him and hide my face in the folds of the back of his jacket. In a flash, we jerked forward and took off across the bridge.

I closed my eyes tightly through most of the ride across the bridge, certain I was going to see our impending deaths. I was content to let JD weave through the cars, the burnt rubble, the horrific bodies and the rotting zombies without a visual. The only reminder of that trip was the smell, but you actually start to get used to it after a while. Keeping my eyes shut may not have been the smartest move I've ever made, but I didn't need any more fodder for my nightmares. To my knowledge, we didn't run into any zombies crossing the bridge.

JD slapped my leg and pointed. I opened my eyes as we passed the toll bridge and there on either side of the streets were such messes as would befit a war movie. Most of the streets had accidents that had long burned out leaving charred skeletons of vehicles, toppled telephone lines that gave no indication whether they were still carrying a charge and abandoned emergency vehicles with their lights off. We'd need a bulldozer to get around all of it, or a motorcycle. I hit him on the shoulder and pointed down one of the streets to our left. About a dozen zombies milled around on a couple of the streets to our left. He nodded and revved the motor speeding us further into the city through the turmoil.

I'd like to say our trip was uneventful, but I'd be lying. We had a nerve-wrecking experience where we rounded a bus into a pack of zombies where the bike skidded out from under us. I cast a few holding spells while JD pulled an ax from the backpack and hacked and slashed until we'd cleared the bike and the immediate area. Another tense moment came when we turned a corner, entered an intersection and found ourselves surrounded. I fired the uzi as JD spun donuts in the middle of the intersection until we found a path out. Each experience was epic and terrifying and each experience was topped only by the following experience.

Eventually we made it to a shopping area near the water. I tried to tell JD that we could shop another time, but he insisted. We barely got off the bike and got started before we were set upon by a horde of zombies in face make-up and a crazy selection of clothes. It sort of ruined the mood, plus the selection was limited to t-shirts and San Fran paraphernalia. We headed out again and found a street lined with little shops with stuff that I would normally pick for myself.

I found a couple of button-up shirts, some jeans that made my ass look great, a soft as butter leather jacket and a new pair of hiking boots. JD kept watch as I tried on a parade's worth of clothes, but we were mostly undisturbed in our shopping experience. We ended up finding and filling two saddle bags for the cycle and a lucky find on a helmet for me. All for the low, low price of nothing.

I'm pretty sure JD got some shopping in too because there was less room available in the bags than I remembered. We might have kept going until dark if I hadn't insisted we stop. Retail therapy is great and all, but I didn't want to risk being on the menu for dinner. The sun was still up and it was clearly early afternoon, but we had to find a place to stop before dark. One thing about the world now is an early curfew and an all too exciting night life. We packed up and prepared to head out.

"My friend lives on Haight Street, in an apartment complex." He strapped his helmet on while checking out the street ahead. Something about that information tugged at my brain. I thought for a moment, and then adjusted my chin strap.

"I haven't seen any indication of survivors around here," I told him. We hadn't either. No signs on buildings or cars, no people sitting by the window pointing guns down at the street, and no sign of barricades or clean up. It was nothing like the movies. All we had was roving bands of ghoulish figures in a somewhat scattered pattern.

I pulled myself onto the cycle. I still objected to travel by motorcycle but I could see the practicality of it. Besides I had a helmet now and if we crashed again I might keep my brains intact enough to pull us out of it.

"Never know. She's a tough one." He mounted the cycle and I jumped on. "If anyone could make it she would. You might even know her. Gloria Schuck."

"Don't recognize the name." I called back. "Is she an old flame or something?"

He applied the brake and put his foot down to turn and look back at me. There was a strange look on his face, one I couldn't read. Had I said something wrong?

"What?" I asked finally.

"She's one of the council's elder members. She's retired, only advises on the serious stuff when it comes up. But she's well known in the magical community." I could feel his gaze, watching my expression. I hoped that the sudden comprehension didn't show on my face.

"Oh, that Gloria. Yeah, Gloria Schuck. Yeah, I've heard of her, can't say I've met her or anything. Just didn't ring a bell when you said it before." I tried to laugh it off but I could hear my voice talking a little too loud and a little too fast. JD didn't respond and his poker face kept looking back at me which made me even more nervous. "She's not someone I'm used to thinking about, ok. I just didn't remember her right off."

His expression didn't change for a moment, then he nodded and turned back to the front and we rolled out again. We moved almost effortlessly and without incident until we got within a couple blocks of Haight Street. All the while I ran the conversation through my head again and again. I could kick myself. Why hadn't I just told him who I was and, well, the truth about myself? Why all the secrets? It's not like the Elders were going to kill me now.

Then there was Gschuck. Could it be that Gschuck wasn't some weird German guy after all, but a funny way of signing her name? Still, the advanced level of spells that Gschuck had worked on add to the new information JD had given me about her being an Elder and on the Council made sense. I started to get a little uneasy.

The signature and penmanship was the only thing besides her spells that I knew about her. If she were hardcore about rogues and the execution policy, or whatever, would she kill me the instant we met? And to complicate things, apparently JD knew her too. In fact, he knew quite a bit about wizards and the Elders. But why hadn't he cast any spells? Was he a wizard? And if he was in with the Council, why didn't he know what I was? The questions occupied my mind, squeezing each other out as they prodded my thoughts.

As we approached the apartment buildings on Haight we had to slow. There must have been a parade or protest or something because the street was packed with the undead. There was so little room we saw several fights break out between zombies as we watched from up the street. There was no way we could handle them all. Not enough ammo, no way that we could spell sling our way through it and it would be a marathon of axe swinging or whatever.

"Hop off." JD unbuckled his chin strap. "Take the saddle bags off, we need to store them."

I got off the motorcycle and worked at the buckles holding the saddlebags to the cycle. JD was looking around, testing the doors, checking out the street. There were a few vehicles that looked operable, but none that would allow us to zoom in and take out or drive over a couple hundred zombies. This was a suicide mission and I was about to say so when the sound of a crack and the bang of a door from my right. JD had found a small closet of a room made of concrete and opened to street level.

JD grabbed the saddle bags from the ground where I'd set them and all but tossed them into the maintenance closet. I walked over, curious about what he was doing. The closet was small, a few pieces of equipment, rakes, electrical and water meters for the housing nearby.

"Get in, don't come out until they're gone." I stared at him, comprehension sinking in even before I saw the handheld horn in his hand.

"No." It was a simple statement. I shook my head. "I'm not going to let you do this."

"You can't stop me. Now get in there and hold the door. They shouldn't bother you but be ready to put down any that lag behind." He handed me a slip of receipt paper with an address scrawled on it. "I'll meet you there. It may take me an hour or so."

He glanced down the street. "Maybe two, just in case."

I moved toward the cycle determined to stop him. I even envisioned myself going with him. He couldn't do this by himself, he'd get himself killed. My arm was pulled back and I was swung around. JD's lips pressed to mine and the warmth and tenderness of his kiss and the soft caress of his tongue sent chills down my body. I moved closer against him, trying to pull

93

him into me despite the danger around us. When he separated I felt a twinge of regret.

If I'd opened my eyes I might've been able to duck. As it was I felt a sharp blow, saw little bursts of light behind my eyelids and sank into darkness. When I woke up I felt the cold concrete beneath me. Disoriented, I sat myself up and groaned at the ache in my jaw. Bastard hit me.

Chapter 8

I crawled to the crack of light under the door, feeling my way around the equipment and the saddle bags. I was about to push it open when I heard the high pitched whine of a motorcycle engine interrupted by the reverberating sound of a loud horn. He passed the door and I clunked my head on the door. Damn it.

If I headed out there now I'd get caught in the wave. My mind raced through the possible solutions. How could I save him? What could I do to keep him alive so I could kill him myself?

The sound of the horn got further away, but the groans and hissing of the undead and the shuffling of feet grew louder. I looked around the closet and realized with more than a little irony that JD had been right. While those zombies making their way down the street could be held out by the door and the concrete, I was stuck inside with no food or water.

To help him, I'd have to help myself. I moved the power washer in front of the door and tried to secure the door with other equipment available to me. Then I sat toward the back and tried to remain as silent as possible. As the shuffling and moans got louder my heart started to beat faster, my muscles tensing. I jumped at the first bump against the door, the rattle of the handle. But the door held. There was no reason for them to come in.

It was sort of like rain battering the door, or at least that's how I tried to picture it. Ignore the gasping, scratching sounds. Ignore the rotted flesh smell and the urge to gag. Ignore the fact that if they detect the stirrings of life in this tiny little room that they wouldn't stop until they satisfied their cannibalistic natures and this place would become my tomb. My tomb in a God damned maintenance closet.

Suddenly the door pushed open a little and a decomposing head with a blood crusted eye socket squeezed through the opening. I held my breath and ever so slowly curled up tighter into a ball in the shadows of my little corner. I could feel my heart beat pounding in the back of my head, almost a headache and my stomach flip-flopped. My mind raced but the only repeating thought was more like a prayer. Go away. Go away. Go away.

The pressure washer slid a little as this thing pressed against the door. An arm and a shoulder joined the head and it scratched at the wall, struggling to get in. I was pretty sure it didn't know I was in here, but if he made it into the room he'd soon find out.

I couldn't shoot them or I'd draw attention to myself. I could use some of the melee weapons but it usually took me more than one blow and the sounds might draw some unwanted attention, although not as much as a gunshot. Neither option suited. I just couldn't risk distracting the zombies and luring them my way without some escape route.

I took a breath and calmed my mind, pulling and beckoning the magic to come to me. I could tune out the sickening sound of nails and bone being dragged across the wall as this thing tried to breach my sanctuary. I could focus beyond the smell of sweat and blood and fear. Concentrate. I needed some way to keep him from wanting to be in here. It had to be something that wouldn't risk burn out this early in the game.

Almost without thinking about it I began to cast my protection spell, this time without the stones. It was not something I'd ever tried before, not seriously anyway, but there was no time for contemplation of consequences. I moved the energy, shaped it into a dome that covered me in my corner.

It didn't take much energy, but there was a small part of my mind that was thrilled and excited that this was working. Usually, I used the stones, but I was beginning to see that it was possible to cast without them. In fact, the stones could be useful for a sustained spell focus while you cast other magic, but was not the only way to make this work. I was building a shelter with only my mind, adding layer after layer of protection.

On a whim I envisioned an avoidance spell that I'd read and tried but never been able to successfully cast. With opposition it's like holding a five pound bucket of water over your head, eventually you're going to get tired and drop it. Still, if I could add some avoidance to the spell I was holding in my mind it would make me feel a little safer. I added a layer of an avoidance spell, as if like a coat of nail polish, coating thinly across the exterior of my dome.

I'm not sure what possessed me or gave me the insight in that moment, but it seemed to be working. Not sure that the layering would maintain or even how many layers I could add, but with my small success I pushed to add more layers. All I wanted was to make my area very quiet and repel this rotted thing from finding me.

The layers seemed to stay in place, at least it felt like it did, and I kept building layer upon layer to increase the thickness of the spells. Necessity is the mother of invention, and maybe that was it. This sort of magic, used in this way, I knew, was one of those all or nothing deals. I just hoped that I had enough karma or miracles or whatever to make this gamble work.

The power washer slid further and the other items I had stacked against the door tumbled to the floor. The thing tumbled into the room, followed by another that peeked in through the now open door. The one on the floor scrambled to right itself, but its movements were jerky and the debris on the floor was hard for it to negotiate. I forced my breath out, using it to focus, calm and direct my concentration on the only best chance I had.

My mind settled a bit from the panicked paths it was prepared to go down and instead began to float outside of the situation, looking down on what was happening as if I were observing a movie and controlling the characters at the same time. As I breathed out I pushed my will into expanding the dome of magic I'd built up, like blowing up a balloon. I felt some resistance, but once I'd applied a certain amount of pressure, the dome expanded little by little. I felt a giddy sort of triumph as I expanded it a little more and a little more again. Please may the avoidance spell work, I thought, even as I pushed the perimeter out enough to press against the first of my two little problems.

I could feel the pressure on my skin, a weird sensation that made me want to rub my arms and pull back. Almost as if a question, without words, I knew I had to decide whether this rotting and rambling corpse was friend or foe. In that moment it was clear that the avoidance spell was working! I rejected the zombie's presence and felt the spell work again as a shove that pushed back against my frame and forced the air from my lungs. It was as if the magic was alive, as if it was some force that was using me as leverage to bolster its kickback against the intruder. The spell bucked in my mind until I could not hold anything but a wisp of the tail end of the spell and it went out from me.

In that moment I realized that there were spells that you didn't have to control and hold in your mind, not completely anyway. Most spells, you form and shape it in your mind and it exists because it is a thought you concentrate on until the spell is done. It is mentally exhausting, but necessary. But this spell was different. There was something of a sentience to this spell and it required some freedom from my mind to work. It was an amazing revelation and I didn't have the time to relish my new found knowledge. And the zombie? It moved back, jerking its limbs as if by reflex to some stimuli that was unseen.

I watched, still maintaining my magic as the thing on the floor shuffled on hands and knees back toward the door. The one standing at the doorway contemplating its further exploration into my sanctuary swung its arm down to attack the one crawling in its direction. They hissed and lunged at each other, but didn't continue to move outside. The last thing I wanted to do was move closer to these two, but the smell was getting so strong that my gag reflex was threatening to destroy my concentration. I directed the spell and the bubble toward the door and slid on my butt a few inches toward the two zombies.

I didn't give myself time to think whether the spell would be strong enough to handle both of them at the same time. It was all or nothing. I inched further, trying to keep some of the debris between me and them, just in case. Yeah, I know it wasn't much of a defense, but it was the only comfort I had to hold onto as I moved toward the door. The first zombie stopped trying to fight and jerked and twisted just get away. The other took advantage of its victory until the boundary of my spell finally reached him.

Again, I was given a choice of friend or foe and again I rejected the presence in front of me. The spell bucked again but I was ready for it and braced myself for impact. There was a hesitation and for a sickening moment I thought that I had pressed my luck. But the spell held and both of them backed slowly onto the street like puppets being carried by their strings. I guess the instinct to fight was harder to resist, but my spell won out.

Adrenaline was still pumping through my system but lowered enough for me to feel the tightness in my chest, the wobbliness of my legs and arms and the numbness in my head. The relief of my success made my eyes water. I collected myself as best I could, knowing that I couldn't lose it then and there. I pushed myself up abruptly, steadied myself and looked around. The room was clear and through the now cleared and open doorway I could see the bodies, jumbled and walking in the direction JD must have driven to lead them out of the area.

I crept slowly toward the door, staying as close to the shadows as possible until I came to the frame of the door. I held the spell between the sidewalk and the doorway I stood in, which was amazingly simple to maintain now that I'd set the thing up. The parade of undead shuffled, dragged and loped past me. The ones that came too close were pushed back by the spell and the rest didn't even glance my way. The kickback seemed to be less and less the more it was engaged with intruders.

I waited until a majority of the parade had gone before I moved further out to the door jamb, trying to see both ends of the street better. It was probably curiosity and security that won over the decision to stay put until JD returned. It helped that I had magic to repel these things, but there was also the close call and bad associations with that little concrete room that kept me from staying. I didn't want to stay in that tomb and I wasn't sure that I would ever have a love of small, dark places again.

With slow determination I hauled our bags out of the room and set them near the door for a quick move to a new location. There were still stumbling bodies, some dragging limbs, others dragging their whole bodies paraded down the street. In the distance I thought I could hear the motor of the cycle and the faint honk of that stupid horn. I stayed as still as possible while assessing the scene.

The protection spell wouldn't prevent them from seeing me, just not make my actions as visible or interesting. Of course, things that interest a zombie are likely to be different from the things that interest most normal people. The spell was made for normal people.

The few zombies that came near hit the avoidance spell and suddenly got confused and seemed to be pulled in a new direction before wandering off. I wasn't really sure how a full targeted attack from one or more zombies would work with the avoidance spell and it seemed safer not to test my luck too much. It was enough for small groups and individuals but not large crowds. I'd been lucky so far and JD's distraction took most of the more physically agile zombies out of the picture.

The few that remained trailing behind the first few waves was pretty beat up and degraded. Most were dragging themselves, missing limbs and looked to be nearing the end of their zombie hording days. I figured they could be run around and avoided and with my spells. There was a chance that they wouldn't follow me to the townhouses and apartments down the street.

The parade slowed and the flow of the bodies had become a trickle. Many of them were still staggering after JD, but the aggression level was up and refocused the remaining zombies against each other. There were still more zombies than I was comfortable handling and I looked around trying to find some way to get them further up the street. Then I heard it.

Up the street, maybe a few blocks away an alarm went off, its screech echoed down the street. The sound, combined with the collective sighs and hisses of the undead, was eerie. It did, however, renew the interest and direction of the group that hadn't made it as far up the street as their predecessors. The zombies that could sped up their pace and headed toward the sound of the car alarm. I stood and watched the continuation of the world's nastiest parade as it filtered passed and swore if I ever found a zombie free location I'd fortify and preserve it. It took about thirty minutes for most of them to pass me by and I swear I heard the faint sounds of a second alarm, although it could have been the resounding echo.

I waited another fifteen minutes to let the last of the stragglers get up the street then dropped my protection spell to conserve energy. I juggled as many of our bags together and slowly made my way down the street. There were a few zombies that just weren't going to make it. Like the woman who looked like she'd been part of a magician's act to cut her in half but forgot to put the bottom half of her back together again. A line of intestine wormed behind her as she struggled to pull herself along. There was only one manicured nail left on her fingers; she'd probably ripped the others off scratching and clawing her way everywhere. I put her out of her misery with a fallen tree limb.

A few of the less brilliant zombies had gotten stuck behind overturned vehicles and debris. They were few enough that I dispatched them as well, conserving my magic to hold onto the avoidance spell in case I ran into any nasty surprises. I juggled the bags and checked the receipt slip JD had given me. One block up and one block over, approximately and I'd be there. I sighed. Part of me would have given anything to see crazy pants again. I just hoped his survival skills matched his ego.

With the exception of day break and night fall, time had less meaning these days. The best way to tell time in a zombie-infested territory is by the number of zombies you have to go through to accomplish something. Like, it took me twenty five zombies to get to the store for some canned goods. Or, it was cold out so it only took eight zombies to get to the police station to scope for ammo. That's the way I counted the time to get to the address JD had sent me to find. Gloria, you better have something worth this risk.

I rounded the first corner and saw that JD had cleared a majority of the street's occupants. There was still a rather large group milling a block or two up, but the threat registered low enough as to not be an immediate problem and high enough for me to acknowledge that I couldn't take out that many by myself without drawing undue attention to myself. I would just have to stay quiet. It took me about a dozen zombies to get from that maintenance closet, which felt so very far away now, to the apartment building I was looking for. My physical fortitude was beginning to wane, so I was glad when the building numbers matched up.

The next problem was that this apartment complex had a system where you either needed a key or you had to buzz the occupants to let you up. It was a single access door, bars on the grunge-covered windows and dried blood covering the number pad. It took quietly taking out another five zombies to find a loading door that had been propped open by a severed hand. It was a double door and looked like it had been used for getting furniture up to the apartments.

Eight more zombies in the entry area and I had the main floor to myself. The windows were just as dirty on the inside as they had been on the outside. After securing the loading door, I found a service door with access to water and electricity meters and a couple of beat up washers and a single dryer. There was a grid of mail slots across from the front entrance, now splattered and smeared with crusted blood. Over near the loading doors, there was an elevator and an open staircase wide enough to walk a couch up to an apartment.

I tightened the straps on my backpack and adjusted the saddle bags to tromp up the stairs. On the first switchback a pile of bodies loomed above me like a wall. Zombies in various states of decomposition lay in an awkward pile between me and the second floor. I could see skulls; faces peeling off, mangled limbs and the stench could have killed someone. My stomach lurched and I almost lost it. Deep breaths and putting my head between my knees for I don't know how long helped me regain my composure.

I brought the bags back down to the entry area and went back up, steeling myself for round two. Nothing seemed to be moving but it was a good indication that someone had survived at least long enough to push the bodies into the stairway. My choice would have been out the window onto the street, but whatevs. It did confirm that we were right to seek out Gloria, though.

Although none of the corpses seemed to be moving, there was no way to tell if they were truly incapacitated. I shuddered to think of climbing this wall, only to be bitten or scratched by one of those zombies that was only missing the limbs to move but still had the undead thing going on. Worse, by the look of the decay if I did try to climb over those bodies, it could be a quicksand situation only I'd never be able to take enough showers in my lifetime or be able to wipe my memory clear of sinking through flesh that oozed out from under me. I shuddered again. Stupid imagination. Not going to happen.

I reached out and tested the handrails. They were still attached to the wall, but they looked thin and possibly rickety. They might not hold my weight if I tried to use them to steady myself and avoid the liquid mess in the middle. The thought occurred to me that if I did need to get out of here quickly, I'd have to come back down through this. Still, I had to try because if Gloria was still alive and with answers it would be worth it all.

Think. Think. Think. If I couldn't make it over, then maybe I could clear it out. I know we had rope, with a bit of leverage from the bottom I could probably pull the pile down the steps a bit. I'd still have to walk over them, but at least I wouldn't have to climb as high or sink as quickly. The only really bad problem with the plan was not only would I be wading through body bits and goo, but the bottom zombies were a bit juicier than the zombies up top. I could be excavating for a bit and I really wanted to get setup in a secure shelter for the night sooner than later. There was no way we'd be getting out of the city before nightfall.

The alternatives were the elevator, a death trap to be sure. And magic. I thought on that one but I didn't really have any spells that would be useful in this situation. I could use fire but I never really had much control over the fire spells I used and I was afraid of setting the building on fire. I mean, getting it started was a pain, but keeping it from burning everything else around it was more than I could handle. Maybe it was my lack of skill but I really think I could overcome it with practice. Problem is, where?

Still, that had a better sound to it than excavating, climbing over and through bodies or scaling the outside of the building and kicking in a window. With my sister, that had been different. She was in a protective circle when I'd cast a fire spell, but I couldn't get a protective circle around and under all these bodies before I cast it which was the real problem with that plan. But I wondered whether that shielding spell could be used to contain the fire. That is, if I could push it around someone else instead of around myself.

I checked my head, mentally inventorying whether I had the energy to pull this off. I didn't feel tired or extended beyond my means so I gathered my will and began to form the protective dome around myself once more. Somehow knowing that I'd done it before, made it easier to cast this time.

When I'd added all the layers I thought might be necessary to contain the fire, I pushed the dome away from me. My hope was to push the center of the dome toward the center of the pile of bodies above me. Since I couldn't see over the edge I had to estimate how far it was. Hopefully I didn't get the wall too much.

The dome moved slowly, almost unwillingly to where I was directing it. As if to tell a loyal attack dog to go away from its master, I struggled to keep it moving until it was positioned over the bodies. It paused and seemed to hold.

Now was the hard part. I considered how to cast my fire spell into a protected area, while holding the protection spell and keeping it in position. I also had no idea if the protected area would keep me from casting the fire spell through the barrier. However, if I carved out the protection in the center then cast fire it should keep the walls from burning and take out a majority of the mess up above.

I pushed my will into re-shaping the dome, but it stubbornly refused. I could feel the tickling of a headache beginning and a cold sweat broke out along my upper lip. I pushed again. Every time I renewed my energy the protective spell would bow slightly then snap back into place. The resistance was eating into my energy and the headache was beginning to bloom. I dropped both spells and slumped to the floor.

Better not to risk burn out right now especially with no one here to help me recover. If I was spending the night down here I'd need the rest of my energy to safeguard this area. I looked up at the mound of zombies then stood up.

"Hey, up there! Can you hear me?" Yeah it was a risk that there might be zombies roving around up there, but I was betting it would be as hard for them to get down to me as it was to get up to them. I listened, but there was no sound or sense of movement.

"I'm a survivor. Is there anyone up there?" I yelled a little louder, cringing at the sound of my own voice bouncing off the walls. There still was no answer.

I grabbed the backpack in one hand and managed to grab both the saddle bags with my other and marched back downstairs. I considered moving to another location before it got too late, but dismissed it. This was the less desirable end of Haight and I knew I'd seen photos of Victorian houses in the more popular areas of San Fran. There was no way JD would be able to find me though, if he survived drawing the zombies out. I sat on the last couple of steps with my head in my hands as I contemplated the miserable night before me.

Chapter 9

As I sat there wondering if I'd see JD again or if he would get trapped somewhere else for the night, I heard the back service door handle rattle. I looked over and sighed. Another damn zombie. I stood up to open the door and blast the thing when the familiar sound of a door lock being picked attracted my notice. JD pushed open the door and strode in, pushing the door closed again.

He looked up at me and smiled. I shook myself clear of the shock and ran to hug him.

"You made it." I whispered, relief flooding me. Then I stepped back and slugged him in the face hitting his cheek. "Don't ever do that shit again."

He rubbed his cheek and gave me a boyish grin. I readied to punch him again, but as my hand flew, he sidestepped the blow and grabbed my arm. I pulled it back and scowled at him. He reached up to touch my jaw where he'd hit me and I winced.

"I can't believe you hit me and then left me in that room, you arrogant son of a—"

"Casey, it was necessary." He started stepping around the lobby floor as he spoke. "It was a calculated risk to get us here and it worked. We're fine."

My head began to throb with all the violence I wanted to unleash upon him in that moment, but a part of me was so relieved that he'd made it back. I let him wander around as I had done, not explaining or speaking until I could trust my voice. He ran up the stairs and then returned a few minutes later.

"Stairs are blocked; looks like we'll be taking the elevator." He walked over and pressed the button as if it had been any other day. The doors slid open and he stepped in. I walked over amazed to see the elevator clean and operational with him holding the door.

"Get in, the alarm will sound if the door is held open too long. We don't need the added attention." I stepped into the elevator, but it seemed surreal, like a dream.

JD must have sensed my amazement because he said casually, "People are conditioned to avoid elevators in emergencies because the likelihood of having difficulties with them is increased during an earthquake or fire. Thing is, it's a liability thing. Most elevators have so many failsafe protocols you could ride them anytime. But the conditioning plays out and even during a zombie invasion, people are likely to avoid them."

I don't know whether it was the stress or just the idea that with zombies around people wouldn't use the elevator, but I started giggling. Hadn't I avoided the elevator for the very same reason?

JD gave me a worried look and put his hand on my shoulder. I shook my head and continued to hold my sides as I vibrated with amusement. It was a good thing the elevator was moving as slowly as it was because it took me a minute to get myself under control. By the time the doors opened to the third level, I'd sobered up a bit, ready for what might be ahead.

The hallway appeared to be cleared out, most likely the work of a survivor clearing this area for habitation. JD looked at me and put his fingers to his lips. We couldn't know how jumpy or volatile anyone we found might be. I nodded agreement and we walked down most of the way down the hall until we came to the apartment number on the slip. The lights in the hallway were still working, but they only covered an arc below each door. The window at the other end provided some light but the building next door was so close that it didn't provide much light at all.

"Casey, watch for movement" he said, lifting his hand. He knocked on the door and waited. The moment was tense and I swear I felt a shift in the air or some sensation of movement, but nothing happened. My nerves were starting to wear me down, I thought. I'll never enter another damn city again.

I moved in front of the door, pushing JD aside, and knocked the familiar pattern of 'shave and a haircut, two bits' the universally accepted code for, 'we're ok, let us in.' We waited for what seemed like forever but nothing happened. I shook my head at JD and started back toward the elevator. We still had time to get a better setup for the night and I'd prefer a bit more style than this dump.

The now familiar crack of another door being kicked in sounded behind me. I dropped my head into my hands and offered the question up to the universe. 'Why, why must he kick in all the doors?' No answer came, so I turned and followed him into the apartment.

"What's up?" I asked dropping into one of the couches.

"Shut the door." He said as he walked toward a desk on the far side of the room.

"With the ruckus you're making I doubt there's a need. They'd be all over us if they were around to hear it." I yawned. The room was nicely furnished, but way too clean. There were bookshelves with knick knacks and collected items. Photos of landscapes and the whole thing was very tasteful but reminded me of my shrink's office.

"Shut it," he snapped. I rolled my eyes and secured the door, then moved into the bedrooms to check things out there. There seemed to be something out of place here but I couldn't quite put my finger on it until I saw the e-book reader on the bed stand. Unless this elder wizard was checking out her magic books from the library there was nothing to indicate that she was living here. It was more like an office or panorama for normalcy.

I walked back into the living room and stood in the middle of the room. JD was searching the desk but seemed to be pulling up only stationary, office supplies, nothing that would indicate a personal life. I knew I was right. But where would she keep her real life, I wondered.

Time for a seeking spell. My searching and seeking spells were finely tuned and well-practiced. They were invaluable for finding rare books and hidden tomes. As a kid there had been a side benefit of always being the one who found the lost keys or sunglasses. It was a treasure trove waiting to happen.

I opened my senses to the spell as I pulled it into a sweeping curve around me, not unlike a tornado only the edges kept pressing outward. It took less than a minute to find an interesting spot against one of the walls near the desk. My eyes could only see a wall there, but I could feel that there was something more. I stepped closer and focused on that feeling. The sensation of some sort of a masking spell glowing faintly in the shape of a rectangle large enough to walk through. I was betting it was a door or a portal to the real home of Gloria Schuck.

The spell was delicate and masterful; I'd not seen or felt anything like it. If there were books behind this door it would be a challenge not to try to grab a few before we left of stuff every bag if Gloria hadn't made it. This was a jackpot and I could only hope that I could get my hands on this spell at least.

"What is it?" I jumped and nearly fell into JD when he whispered into my ear, his breath warm against my skin.

"Hold on." I sent the seeking spell toward the door again, trying to find a weakness or trigger to allow us to pass. A banana split sounded excellent, I thought. I bet there's an ice creamery just up the street. I needed something cool and creamy. The half frozen banana was an added bonus. I'm an old fashioned girl with the chocolate, strawberry and vanilla.

JD grabbed my arm and asked, "Where are you going?" I looked at him blankly, reality filtering slowly back to me. Oh yeah, no ice cream, only zombies. Disappointing.

"Damn, she's good." I smiled appreciatively. I hadn't even sensed the avoidance spell. Maybe I'd triggered it when I'd probed the door with my seeking spell, but I suspected it had been layered under another spell. Tricky, but oh so good. I crossed the room back to the door.

"Maybe we can find another way in," he asked looking at me. I shook my head.

"My bet is that this is the weaker link. We may not find the other doors. This is a secret entrance, a quick path she uses between her office and home." I waved my arm across the room. "The reason this place is so tidy, the furniture is just so and there are no personal effects is because this is a sitting room or office, maybe. She probably entertains guests here, nothing more. No use people seeing what you're really up to."

I looked back at the door and applied the what-would-I-do-here situational thinking to the problem. Then inspiration struck. I didn't need to search the whole door; I'd just look for the handle. It was simple enough to be genius. Anyone who searched for something other than that would find themselves somewhere else and not sure what they were doing just before it. But a quick entry into and out of the door would just require knowing what to look for as well as where to look.

Turning, I grabbed JD's hand. "Don't let go of my hand. No matter what happens, what you feel, just keep your thoughts on holding my hand, ok?" He nodded.

I cast the seeking spell again but this time I sought the door handle in the middle of the door. I could feel the resistance but not the kickback of the avoidance spell. A slow insidious building of fear and uncertainty filled me. This avoidance spell was top notch; I had to get me one of these. I pushed forward, reaching for the handle.

Cold sweat broke out all over my body and my vision narrowed to tunnels when I grabbed the handle and turned. My breath was quick and shallow as I pushed with everything I had while pulling a now struggling JD. Maybe I should turn back now. This was worse than crawling over dead bodies, worse than having to hide my magic and being denied training. This was worse than watching my sister slowly succumb to this atrocity.

The avoidance spell probed my fears and my uncertainty, expertly manipulating and cajoling me into leaving. It might have worked, I might not have been able to withstand the slow building pressures, but when it had touched upon my sister's death it had tread upon something more important than fear and uncertainty. At the thought of my sister I sobered and my resolve and defiance increased until the pressure was bearable. I threw myself through the doorway into the unknown and my grip on JD became steel despite his struggles. The stinging sensation overtook me, hundreds upon thousands of biting, stinging points on every inch of my body. I fell fighting to breathe.

When I took my next breath there was a cool musty sensation in the air. The phantom stings hovered in my memory and I freed my hands to rub them over my skin. There was no blood or welts, but they still felt real. I heard JD wheezing next to me, felt his body heaving as if he'd run a marathon. I reached over to touch him and felt his shirt, sweat soaked and his body shivering. The room we were in now was dark but it felt small. Panic at the thought of being back in that concrete tomb spurred me to act.

I reached out blindly, trying to feel my way to the light. My defenses were down, my mind was numb from the resisting the avoidance spell. I pushed the doors open and they moved freely on the rails at the top and bottom of the closet doors. The lights were still off, but there was a curtained window with soft early evening light peeking at the bottom. I crawled forward without a thought of what might be in this room. I just wanted to be in the light again. There was too much darkness in my world right now. Suddenly my wish was granted.

Light opened up in the room, no source that I could detect, and no specific direction. We were in a small bedroom with no pictures or knick knacks or furniture of any kind. The window, the closet and a door were the only things besides us. I looked over at JD who was attempting to stand and having difficulty keeping his balance.

"I think I triggered the light spell when I moved forward." I said pushing myself up. "You ok?"

"Are there any more booby traps?" He nodded toward the door

"I don't think so. We made it through her defenses. This should be the inner sanctum." I looked around, trying to sense any danger that might indicate otherwise. "Depending on how she ran business, I suspect that anyone who didn't know what she was would leave without searching a wall. And, anyone who did know would have to deal with those defenses. Besides, there're probably alarms that would alert Gloria and then they'd have more problems than just the spells."

"It's possible that the spell has degraded a bit since she last cast it, too." He flipped the curtain back enough to sneak a peek at the street below. "We might not have been able to withstand the intensity of her spell had it been stronger."

"You mean it could've been worse?" I asked. JD turned and looked at me, frowning.

"Is there something you want to tell me?" His voice was low, calm and dangerous. I swallowed hard and tried to fake a smile.

"I don't know what you mean." I took a half step back, but he followed me with two large steps of his own, backing me half way into the closet.

"Enough with the games." JD said. "You're lying, and you're bad at it. There isn't a wizard around who doesn't instinctively know the name

Gloria Schuck. And, it's second level spell training to know that spells fade and need upkeep. You're way past the age to have learned about this. I don't know what your deal is but I'm tired of the lies. Our lives depend on trusting each other and I think I've more than proven myself to you. Now, tell me the truth. Who are you, who is your master and why don't you--"

I don't know why tears sprang to my eyes. If I could have gone back in time to have my tear ducts surgically removed, I would have. Blinking and trying to focus on something other than the warm smell of him, I stood there looking at the carpet and feeling stupid.

"You're a rogue, aren't you?" His voice was softer this time and I looked up to see that his expression had returned to boyishly handsome. "You don't have a master. You were never trained. But why look for Gloria Schuck? She'd be forced to execute you."

I shrugged, not trusting my voice. He took my shoulders and shook me, my teeth clanked together painfully.

"I found a book, some magic spells by Gschuck." I could feel my face getting red as I talked. "If anyone could help me, help my sister, I thought... There was an address in one of the books. I have to get my sister back. I figured that zombies trump illegal practicing of magic."

My throat locked up and a tear escaped and made its way down my cheek. He caught it with a finger, then smudged the wet line with his thumb. He bent his head down to mine and caught my lips in a delicious kiss, one hand on the back of my head and the other circling my waist. It lasted too long and not long enough. When he pulled away, he seemed to be about to say something.

"Let's get going." He pulled away from me and walked to the door, opening it with a slight hesitation and let the door swing open.

The hallway was dark, with an open door into what looked like another bedroom to our right, a bathroom in the middle of the hall with a closed door across from it and the faint outline of living room furniture toward the very end. JD reached for the light switch and flooded the area with more light.

The open door showed a room that was once a bedroom but had become a small library or study. Bookshelves were lined up on every wall, leaving only an opening for the closet door and the door into the next room. My pulse raced as it does every time I encounter a stash of books. I pushed passed JD and started looking through titles.

Oh. Emm. Gee.

"Jackpot." I whispered to myself as I flipped the light on in that room. JD looked at me and shook his head then continued through the hall to the other door, the closed one.

"Before you start looting, we should be sure that no one else is here." He called over his shoulder. He was right of course, but all I could think about was how to fit all these books into my bag. Maybe we could stay here a few days. I mean, I'm sure there are supplies we could scavenge. Hee! Maybe some sort of generate food spell or something.

I heard him open the door down the hall and reluctantly left my new-found treasure stash to move up behind him. We'd talk books later. Everything was dead quiet. He flicked the switch and the room suddenly lit up. A bedroom, covered in scattered clothes, crystals, odd books and the comforts of a real home. Not a clean one, but Gloria probably found it comfy. No sign of life in this room.

While he made sure there wasn't a boogie man in the closet, I turned to the partially open bathroom door. Even as I opened the door, I sensed something wrong. I turned on the lights to the narrow bathroom. There in the bathtub was a decayed body slamming its fists against an invisible wall. Her hair was whitish grey and her figure looked near skeletal in her zombie state. From the looks of things she'd sealed herself into a barrier spell before she'd turned. She'd need help getting out. That wasn't going to happen.

I heard the muted growl and grunts as she threw herself against the barrier again and again. Her milky white eyes stared at me, her jaws worked uselessly. There must have been a silence spell of some sort, but if spells faded it would eventually fade along with all her other spells. I tried to recognize her from that fateful meeting I'd had with the Elders so long ago, to remember if she'd been there. But recognition did not come.

JD came part way in then wrapped an arm around my waist to pull me out of the way. I held the door jamb and pulled myself back into that bathroom.

"It's ok. She can't get out of there. Not without me breaking the barrier spell she has keeping her in the bathtub." His grip loosened but I could feel him staying close to my back.

On the floor of the bathroom was an array of stones with runes carved into them placed strategically around the tub area to reinforce the spell despite the caster's will being gone. The runes looked interesting but I didn't want to alter anything in case there were contingency spells or other traps. Also on the floor was a journal fallen from the toilet lid where a gold laminate pen lay. The journal lay splayed with a few pages bent from the landing. I walked over and tucked the journal into the back of my jeans.

What was left of Gloria threw herself, body and everything, against the barrier, but the magic held. I walked back to the door, weaving behind JD who stood a couple feet away from her forcing me to walk behind him. When I got to the door he turned and closed the door behind me. I listened at the door then turned away when I realized he was relieving himself.

The only space left to explore was the living room, faintly illuminated by the hall light. After JD secured the bathroom, we walked toward the living room together. For the most part, I wasn't really concerned about other occupants. They would have charged us once the light in the hall was turned on, but it didn't hurt to be cautious. JD moved in front of me, feeling for the switch.

When the lights came on it was like looking into one of those movie style mad scientist dens. There weren't liquids bubbling or anything, but there were books open, test tubes and Bunsen burners everywhere. There were stacks of containers with powders and jars with plant and animal specimens. It was the coolest place I'd ever seen. If there hadn't been a library with forbidden books to read down the hall I might have frolicked through the tables and shelves like a kid at an amusement park.

The kitchen was clearly empty and the front door was locked. Though I was dying to get at the books in her library, I searched the kitchen and looked through the cupboards to see whether there were any supplies available. It would be nice if we could stay here for a night or two, but once I'd scouted the food options, I knew that we'd have to leave the next day. What few provisions would have to be carried back to the backpack and saddlebags we'd left in the office apartment.

I put the food on the counter for JD to pick through, and then sifted through the workstations Gloria had setup. I found a couple of zombie bits, some hypodermics and slides for magnifying them. It looked like Gloria was hunting for a solution but hadn't lived to see it through. Maybe the journal would have more information about that.

Since there were no chairs in the living room, I moved back to the library and settled myself down in the most comfortable armchair I could find. The journal appeared to be a personal accounting of things Gloria was involved with. Fascinating, but maybe something a bit more relevant, Gloria. I flipped ahead to a date closer to the initial outbreak.

The Elders had had two meetings about what was going on, convinced that it was some sort of dark magic. There wasn't time for more than that as the attendance was inhibited by quarantine procedures and infection rates among their own ranks. They had assigned tasks to find the source of the magic so they could counter the effects. Elder Schuck had felt that all eyes had been upon her for a solution and though she'd contributed a lot to wizard kind, she felt that there were some who were disappointed that she didn't have a ready answer for the problem.

I skimmed ahead since it looked like they'd experimented with spells and magic, like I'd done only with more collected magic books between them. No details on the spells, just names and references, so what good was it to me. Gloria seemed to have objected to the experiments shortly after they'd begun. She seemed to think that it was a waste of time, since addressing the problem with magic was likely every trained wizard's first instinct.

With numbers dwindling and options for travel and resources becoming more and more scarce, the Elders had to search for other, less conventional answers. The existing spells weren't working and none of them could find a reason for bodies to walk without a controller, a necromancer to direct their will. The sickness spreading across the world acted like an infection, spreading from one person to the next, but it had to have an origin point. It seemed to start from everywhere all at once. Gloria noted an interesting observation that the souls were being tied to the body, that the infected didn't exactly die. Interesting. I wonder how she came to that conclusion.

"What are you reading?" Startled to have the silence broken, I looked up to see JD holding a couple cans of food.

"Journal. The one I found in the bathroom." I closed the book and stuffed it into the back of my jeans again. "Just curious. They were working on finding the source, so they could, you know, cure it or fix it."

"I'm guessing it didn't work." He tossed one of the cans in the air and it flipped before he caught it. "We should try to find a bag to carry some of this stuff."

I looked around at the books and nodded. I needed these books. Needed like a man on fire needs a pond to jump into. This was an opportunity of a lifetime. There were spell books that I would never have gotten to see in this lifetime and they were just here for the taking. The older ones were way more advanced and complex than I could work, for now, but I'd always persevered before. I sat down to sift through the useful, the really useful and the steep learning curve books Gloria had inadvertently left to me.

Chapter 10

There were no clocks in here, but it felt like I had only just begun when JD cleared his throat to get my attention. I had a stack of books in my hand that I just had to have and they nearly tumbled to the floor when I turned to see what he wanted.

"We should find a place to hole up. It's dark out." I raised my eyebrow at him, and then looked down at my books. These would have to do. I could always come back, right?

"I'm not done yet," I whined.

"You've been at it for hours, babe. It's time to go." He walked over and took half the stack of books in his arms and walked back into the hall. "We need to get setup for the night and our bags are unsecured in the next room. We need to go."

I cuddled the remaining books to my chest and took one last, longing look at all the books I was being forced to leave behind. We wouldn't be back and I knew it, but I couldn't face that truth. I told myself that I would drop back by in the morning to have a final look through, then I walked out into the hall to join JD. He'd made a makeshift sack out of a sheet and had various objects clicking around as he swung it up to his shoulder.

He reluctantly opened the sack and allowed me to put in the last couple of books before hoisting it back up onto his shoulder. JD headed for the only door in this place we hadn't checked, the locked front door. He pressed his ear against the door and waited. When he undid the locks and walked out I saw him enter the hallway we'd come in, but he looked back through the door with a puzzled look on his face.

She was good. I walked through the door, pulling it behind me. I wasn't half surprised to see that the door was gone and a blank wall in its place. I put my hand to the wall, trying to feel the door, but it was just smooth wall. There wasn't even a blank space in the wall to indicate that there should be a door there. I couldn't even sense where the door was. She was very, very good.

JD didn't look back. He just flicked a flashlight on and headed toward the office apartment. He all but tossed the sack of books and food onto the couch I'd sat on when we had first entered this apartment. In the hours I'd been pouring over books it had become pitch black outside the window. We decided to stay in the apartment tonight and leave in the morning.

Our food supply was low, so we agreed to hit the apartments for supplies before we could make camp for the night. First though, we secured the windows, drawing the blinds, then the curtains and finally duct taping the edges of the curtains down so no light could escape. It wasn't fool proof, but we weren't exactly going to have the brightest of lights.

When we'd secured the living room, kitchen and bedroom windows I set about placing my stones and creating a protective barrier in the apartment. I was eager to see if the avoidance spell could be used, but as much as I liked my new spell I had to wait until after we'd done our shopping.

It took an hour to scour the apartments on the floor we were staying on, being sure to take advantage of unsoiled blankets, extra pillows, shampoo and soap and even an extra toothbrush still in its packaging for the unexpected guest. The pickings for food were slimmer than at Gloria's apartment. We'd have to spread out a bit more.

JD argued that we could cover more ground if we split up, one of us heading upstairs and the other down a floor. I argued that that was exactly what the stupid teenagers in horror movies do before they get brutally murdered. To which he replied that if we were stupid teenagers we would be having a lot more sex. I countered with a dirty look and he rolled his eyes and motioned us toward the elevator. We'd start down a floor.

It became a routine. He'd kick the door in; I'd check the window to see whether we'd attracted too much attention. He'd raid the kitchen and come up with maybe an opened package of noodles or a box of crackers. This place really had been picked clean which made me think that there were survivors here, but maybe they'd succumbed as Gloria had.

Half way down the hall, JD kicked the door as usual, but strangely the door didn't budge. He looked at me and motioned me to step back a bit. I bit my lip and waited to see what would happen next. To my surprise, he knocked.

There was no answer, but that didn't mean anything. He yelled at the door.

"Hey let us in. We're like you. We need help. Please, open the door." A faint clicking sounded from within the apartment. JD held his hand up and motioned me to edge closer to the wall. We didn't know this person; we didn't know what kind of people were in there.

When the door finally opened a skinny man with dark rimmed glasses and hairy arms peeked out the door. He looked JD up and down, and then glanced down the hallway at me. I did my best to look as non-threatening as possible, which was easier since I was hauling the food findings in a pillow case. He stepped out, blocking the entrance into the apartment.

"Where did you come from?" His voice was nasal and higher pitched than normal. I bet he caught hell in school. He was dressed in slacks that were torn at the bottom and his shirt and top of his pants were stained the familiar brownish color of dried blood.

"I'm from New York. She's from Marin. We were just passing through, looking for survivors, food, supplies, whatever we can find." JD smiled and opened his hands in a gesture that was meant to instill confidence. The man gave him a wary look then a questioning glance at me. I guess he didn't like the scavenging bit.

"I mean, what're you doing here?" His voice went up an octave and I winced.

"Look we were checking out the city. This looked like a good place to stop." JD stepped back to give the guy a bit more room. I was waiting for the kick to the head but it seemed he was waiting.

"Before I can let you inside, I need to see if you've been bitten." I noticed he looked a bit longer at me when he made the request.

"Sure. Sure." said JD. "As long as we can check you out as well."

The man looked taken aback, looking back and forth between JD and me. It was clear he hadn't considered that he would have to play show and tell, too. There was something in his eyes that I just couldn't read, and instinctively it made me a little nervous. He stepped out of the way of the apartment and waved us both in.

"As long as you're willing, I guess you ain't been bit yet. Can never be too careful, you know." JD grunted as he walked into the apartment. I followed and was met with the unpleasant stale smell of a place where people have been camping too long without showering. The floor was covered with clothes and empty jars and cans. There was a burnt area in the carpet where it looked like someone had tried to build a fire.

A quick scan told me all I needed to know. This was a lair, a cocoon he'd wrapped around himself. He'd raided everything around him but was so attached to the perceived safety of the apartment that he'd locked himself in here. There was a good chance that he wouldn't leave, even if it meant starving to death. There seemed to be no other people, but I couldn't be sure because there were pillows and blankets on the floor, deceptively creased and thrown down.

"Is there anyone else here?" I asked, trying to keep my voice mild and friendly.

He stared at me then looked around. "There were others, but they went out and haven't come back. I expect them back soon so don't go getting any ideas." He walked across the room stepping carefully around the debris on the floor.

"Did they go for food and supplies?" JD asked. He was looking at me as he asked but the skinny guy didn't notice as he was busy kicking a blanket out of his path to the window.

"Yeah, thought they could find more than what was here. I told them it was suicide but they wouldn't listen." He looked back at us. "Said they would die if they stayed here. I saw a couple of them a while ago, but the zombies have gone now so maybe…"

He turned back toward the window as his voice trailed off. JD twirled his finger around his ear. As if I couldn't tell the guy was unhinged. He'd need to be watched, but more likely we'd be convincing him to travel with us. I mean, we couldn't just leave him here to die, now could we.

"So, the pile of zombies in the stairwell, was that you?" I asked walking toward the kitchen area. The carpet crunched under foot and I realized the damned thing was packed with dried blood.

"No, well, yeah. Sort of I guess." He turned suddenly on me. "Do you guys have food with you? Because I don't have any here."

I took a step back. I pulled out one of the cans of soup and put it on the counter for him. I could see JD scowl, but he didn't say anything. The man leapt over to the can and cuddled it in his arms like a baby.

"Look man, we're leaving tomorrow and there's likely to be more food out there. You want to come with?"

In the end Brad declined to search the building with us. It was probably because he'd already scavenged most of the building beforehand. I also suspected he was starving and didn't want to share the soup we'd given him. It was understandable, polite society doesn't really have a place when you've trapped yourself inside a building with limited resources and been surrounded by the horde waiting to eat you if you peeked out the door. He didn't look real physically endowed, so maybe he wasn't much of a fighter either. That pretty much meant we had to take him with us when we left.

I'm not sure if it was light headedness from lack of food or trust issues, but Brad couldn't or wouldn't give us any information about the building or the area in general. He seemed to fade in and out of coherency and after a few minutes JD gave up on him and pulled me away. My opinion was that he hadn't been affected by the virus, but he wasn't all there either. In his own way, I guess, he told us he'd searched the building top to bottom for food, but not much else. We were hoping he'd been wrong.

An hour later the building had been searched and the three of us were in the office-apartment of Gloria preparing dinner. We'd found a box of macaroni and cheese and added a cracker topping for crunch. JD portioned it out equally despite the disappearance of the soup we'd given Brad. We ate in silence except when Brad got up to check the pot for seconds. When he saw that there were none he proceeded to run his fingers around the inside of the pot then licking them.

Eventually, Brad went into the bathroom giving JD and I some privacy. I started the avoidance spell on the outer edges of the protection spell already in place as quickly and as quietly as I could. It was coming faster to me now the more I practiced. Very exciting stuff for a wizard, but maybe not so much for anyone else.

I heard rattling of the toilet handle and figured I had some time left over while Brad did his thing in the bathroom. I hauled the backpack, saddle bags and the rest of the food, books and other things we'd collected from Gloria's bag and put them into the corner between the desk and the secret door-wall. JD nodded consent and I pulled out four more stones and placed them around the pile and cloaked them under another protection spell laced with avoidance for good measure. Brad may have been the only person we'd found so far, but there was something about the glassy-eyed stare when asked certain questions, the leering looks I willfully ignored and the way he kept in eye contact with our bags that made me feel a little uncomfortable. I just didn't trust him. Maybe that would change with time.

JD grabbed the e-book from the other room and I pulled out Gloria's journal. We were both sitting comfortably on the couch reading when Brad returned to the room. His eyes narrowed as he looked around the room searching for what was different. He looked at the spot where our bags had been and then through all the rooms, including the kitchen and all its cabinets. The more he searched the angrier he got. While I felt bad that perhaps I'd inspired one more reason not to trust us, secretly I was glad that our stuff was secure.

"What are you looking for, bud?" JD asked casually.

"Nothing," Brad snapped. He stormed back into the living room and threw himself into a recliner, staring at us unhappily. I ignored him and continued to read about Gloria's efforts to find a cure.

I was soon caught up in the research they'd been doing, well, what news had made it into Gloria's hands. The Elders were not only stumped but the sheer panic came across as they realized that they were out of time. They were losing members to the virus too quickly and they couldn't collect the resources they needed fast enough.

Gloria, meanwhile, had been trying a different tact. She and another wizard living in Oregon had had the idea of trying new spell combinations. Typically when combining spells you pick two spells that are similar, simple and easy to cast so that when you combine them you aren't doing calculus in your head to keep everything tied together and balanced. The last few pages seemed to indicate that they'd tried a combination of advanced level spells so complicated you'd almost need a computer program to run the spells and had found a potentially striking solution to the problem.

Between trying to find an answer, which took up most of her time, Gloria spoke of other survivors in her building, working together to stay alive. I couldn't put the journal down and more than once looked up at Brad to imagine him as part of that group. Apparently there had been some sort of raiding party that Gloria hoped to convince to collect some new materials for her for a few spells that could help get herself to Oregon.

Later, the pages lost the neat penmanship that I'd come to know of Gloria. She'd sustained injuries by an infected soul, as she called them, and even as she was dying she continued to work on getting information north to her friend and colleague. I felt a lump in the pit of my stomach as I read on, seeing in my mind's eye the deterioration as she pushed on, not unlike that of Sophie.

When there was nothing left that was legible, I closed the journal and looked across the room to the blinds covering the windows. She'd taken all the food she'd had, all the supplies she could spare and given them to the survivors in this building when she knew that she wasn't going to make it. She'd done the responsible thing and locked herself away. Something had happened, an attack or something and she'd been infected. As much as I resented the Elders, I couldn't condone that sort of death. But then, neither could I help her.

"You ready for bed?" JD asked softly. I looked at him then nodded. Might as well, I could use the comfort.

Brad volunteered to sleep on the couch, leaving us the bed. As soon as I crawled between the covers, curled up in JD's arms, I fell asleep. I dreamed of her again.

Chapter 11

"Hey Hard Case." Sophie said, standing on the rocks near the bay and looking out over the water. Again the sky, hills and water were monochromatic shades of grey. Everything, except for her.

"Soph, what are you doing here?" I stepped closer to her, but didn't approach the shore. I didn't want to be sucked down into the water again.

"You have to move fast, Casey. You have to make things right again." She turned to look at me and she smiled a brilliant smile. She reached out and tugged on a lock of my hair. "You can do this, Case, I know you can do it."

"Do what, Sophie? Survive?" My eyes flickered back to the path I'd walked from the car to get to the bay. "I hardly feel like I'm doing that anymore. There isn't anyone around, well, except for this guy. But Sophie, there's nothing I can do. The world is dead and I'm not sure I'm strong enough to go on."

"You always were stubborn, Hard Case." She looked at me and I wanted to wrap her in my arms and never let go. I wanted to bring her back. "You have to focus on you, not on me. I'm ash, remember."

"It shouldn't have been you though." I sulked.

"Casey, you don't have time for this. Do you remember when we were kids and I asked you how God stops the tornados?"

I laughed. "Yeah, you were quite the sucker back then." She laughed with me but her eyes stayed serious.

"The tornado has almost run its course here. You need to untwist it before it gets to the end of the road. Find James Willaker, unmake the deal."

The name sounded familiar, but I couldn't place it. I opened my mouth to ask her who James Willaker was when I found myself surrounded by water and being pulled closer to the swirling water in the center of the bay. Not again, I thought.

I turned away from the vortex and tried to swim with everything I had, but the current was too strong and my arms felt heavy and tired. I was spun toward the spiral of death and I could see the silent screams of people already caught in the folds twisting passed me so fast I couldn't make out all their features. I couldn't end like that. Claws reached out, hoping to hook onto something solid and I fought with all the strength I had left to pull myself from this fate for just a few minutes longer.

"Casey, wake up. You have to hurry." Sophie's voice rang out in my head.

I jolted awake, my eyes glazed and taking in the dark shapes in the room. I pushed the covers back when I realized that something felt very wrong. Warning bells went off in my head. I felt JD's warm body resting comfortably next to mine and I tried to catalog what the problem was. Suddenly a looming shadow from the center of the room moved and I knew.

I reached behind me, watching the shape as I moved, and clicked on the lamp. Brad stood there, blinking in the sudden light, one of the long slender kitchen knives in his hand. I threw back the covers and pushing against JD to wake him. Brad charged the bed, his knife arcing down to slash into JD.

"Where is my food? You stole it. You bitch. You stole my food. You're going to die." His words were slurred and angry. Most of them I couldn't make out.

I'm not sure how I was able to pull the magic to myself so quickly, but I moved my hand and cast a holding spell on him before the knife could make contact. The crazed look in his eyes was horrifying to see. JD rolled out from under the knife and grabbed his wrist and snapped it back in a sickening crunch, wrenching the knife from his grasp. I released the spell and Brad, finally able to move, howled in pain. They struggled for a second before JD got in the final punch that sent Brad to the floor.

"Still want to take him with us?" JD said through gritted teeth. I shook my head.

It had seemed humane to take him with us, especially considering that we would be leaving him to a death sentence what with the zombies outside and no food left in the building. Noble as it was to try and save him, he was unstable, violent and too dangerous to risk trusting him again. We'd have to leave him some food of course, but leave him we would.

JD was pulling the tape off the curtains and the blinds and sunlight poured into the room. It was time to get out of here anyway. I joined him at the window and looked down at the street. It was still mostly clear from yesterday afternoon's parade, just a few wanderers who had migrated from up the street. Our bags were packed from the night before, but we'd need to find some way of getting our new found treasures out of here.

I took the spells off the bags and the room and tucked the stones safely away. We made several trips to the elevator to get our stuff down to the first floor. With that done I cast the cover spell again, on the bags only, and checked on Brad. He was still laid out in the bedroom where we'd left him. I checked his pulse and he seemed to be breathing so I left him to sleep it off. JD was pulling on his jacket when I got back to the living room.

"I don't want to stay here any longer than we need to, so is there anything else or anyone else we need to visit while we're here?"

"Not here. Gloria mentioned a wizard up in Oregon. His name is JW according to the journal. Do you know him?" I patted my jeans for the journal to show him the pages when I realized I'd already taken it downstairs.

"Not sure. I might have an address back at my house that could help." It was then that I noticed that he had the motorcycle keys in hand.

"Not again." I groaned. "There aren't that many of them out there. You don't have to keep risking your life doing this."

"Listen, there's no way we can carry all the stuff we've collected to the Hummer on the cycle, but there may be an alternate transportation option." I looked at him and sighed. "I don't want to have to knock you out, babe, so just believe me that it'll be better for both of us if you stay here until I get back. I won't be long and then we'll get out of here."

I walked him downstairs and secured the door behind him. We didn't exchange another word and wouldn't until he returned. I listened for the sound of fighting while he cleared the street, maybe the sound of that damned horn, but I didn't hear anything until a few minutes later when he started up the cycle and drove off.

When I could no longer hear the sound of the motor, I returned to the apartment and plopped onto the couch to wait. I had snagged the journal from our bags while I was downstairs and flipped open to the fated last few days of Gloria's life and re-read them again. Something was bugging me about it. She had made mention of rain in the north and Oregon and a wizard who was always referred to by his initials, JW. My fingers played with my sister's locket as I tried to piece together what was bothering me. Inspiration came in a flash and suddenly I knew.

It couldn't be, could it? Was JW, James Willaker? The dream came back to me. Sophie had told me to find James Willaker, but how had she known? I was pretty sure I didn't have the gift of premonition and I was damned sure I'd never heard of a James Willaker before. At least I thought I was sure. How could my subconscious know his name from a set of initials?

I immediately started rationalizing because the alternative was giving me goose bumps. Maybe I'd heard the name before in underground circles or something. He could have written a few spells and I'd never caught onto the name before. Feeling like there was a solid explanation for this, I put the journal into the back of my jeans again.

I stood up to stretch and dismiss the uneasiness I felt about what I'd just discovered. I walked around the room and into the bedroom for lack of a better place to go. The spot where Brad was laying was now empty. The floor was cool to the touch when I felt the carpet and deduced that he had been gone for more than a few minutes. He hadn't walked past me while I'd been reading, so he must not have been completely knocked out when JD and I had gone downstairs to say our goodbyes.

I searched the apartment, looking in even the most ridiculous of places like the bottom cupboards in the kitchen, but found no trace of him. That wasn't good. I could search all the rooms on each of the floors, but it would be difficult to know whether he'd moved into a spot I'd already searched. Besides, who knew what sort of psychosis the search for him would trigger. He was already violent, and the idea that he was being hunted might push him beyond any sort of reason and inspire even more violent behavior. Until JD showed up my options weren't spectacular. I decided to get to a more defensible position downstairs.

When I got near the door where our stuff was stashed, I entered the protection circle I'd cast for the bags sat in the corner watching for signs of movement. It didn't take long before I heard what sounded like yelling coming from outside. I pushed the front door open a crack and looked out to see Brad screaming at the top of his lungs at the zombies up the hill from us. And they

were taking an unhealthy interest in his show.
Crap.

JD would be back soon but we wouldn't have
any time to load stuff up. I acted before I'd
even really thought about it. I dropped the cover
spell on our pile of stuff and grabbed the sheet
with all the stuff collected at Gloria's, put on
the backpack and grabbed one of the saddle
bags. I ran out the back door and raced to the
maintenance closet. I threw the stuff down,
pulled the door shut and ran back again. As I
got close to the building I noticed that the
biggest mob was about half a block away. I
bolted inside, grabbed the other saddle bag and
the pillow case with the food and ran back
outside to see Brad sprinting back to the
building.

Our eyes locked on one another and he froze in
his tracks to point and scream at me in a primal
sort of way. That was his last mistake as the
zombies who were moving a bit faster than he'd
anticipated caught up with him. They knocked
him down as he swung wildly at them and was
overwhelmed by the rest as they swarmed him.
I thought back to the things Brad had said and I
wondered if he hadn't done this very same thing
before to cause the mob outside the building.
Had he intentionally drawn attention to the
other survivors when they'd gone out for food?
If so, karma's a bitch and it was his turn to pay
up.

While the horde was ravenously feeding on Brad, I ran back to the maintenance closet and dropped the rest of our gear where we could access it easily. I was thinking about getting our stuff away from the feeding pack as quickly as possible and wasn't paying attention. When I turned around to scope the area, I found I had attracted about two dozen zombies who were bearing down on me. There were about a dozen too many for me to handle on my own, so I decided to run for it and hope that none of them camped out near our gear.

I crossed the street and climbed the steps up to a nondescript building. It looked like the front door entrance into an older style house with no signs of movement through the little windows in the door. The wood looked like it would splinter pretty easily, which would be good for entrance but bad for securing against the zombies pursuing me. Besides, I needed them away from the maintenance closet so we'd have to go on a little chase.

I looked back to see how my followers were doing at keeping up. All of them were mobile, but more than half of them were stumbling around on wobbly legs. I might be able to run circles to get away from them. The rest were a little fresher and steadier on their feet. The only problem with running circles is you have to have everyone running at the same pace or you catch up to them with tragic results.

I jumped down the steps, veered right where there was a cement path around the side of the house and to the six foot fence of a side yard. I fumbled with the handle and opened the gate as the first couple of zombies rounded the corner of the house. Everything was going according to plan.

There were some overgrown rose bushes that blocked my view of the yard. I kept quiet and focused my senses to get some sort of indication of what was ahead. It's no good to run into a bigger group than the one you're running from, but the zombies pursuing me were hissing and making too much noise for me to determine what was ahead. I ran forward, pushing the rose bush stems out of my way and found a zombie in a lounge chair with the mostly eaten carcass of a child pulled onto its lap.

You ever see something that makes you just stop what you're doing no matter how important your task is and just stare? It was such an unexpected sight, so horrific and simple. Had the mother or father thought to comfort their child only to succumb to infection or had the child sought the protective embrace of an adult not recognizing the peril? It just took me a moment to process that what I was seeing was real.

That little moment almost cost me my life. As the zombies chasing me burst through the rose bushes and the zombie in the lounge chair lurched for me and rolled the remains of its last meal onto the cement pad, I felt the puff of air as clawed hands swiped at me and missed. I was forced to jump back, sprint across the yard and throw myself up and over the concrete wall along the back. The scrapes of bone on stone sounded as they scratched at the wall where my legs had been a fraction of a second before.

I fell awkwardly to the ground on the other side and was winded. If there had been anything waiting for me back here, I would have been done for. I was in a flower bed of the adjoining yard. There were four zombies lazing about in the house, with the glass doors to the back of this house yawning open. They didn't react to my presence and it seemed that something was going to go right today.

I moved as quietly and quickly as I could toward another six foot wood fence and listened for sounds of unlife. I couldn't hear anything and decided to try my luck at climbing over. Now, unless you're a gymnast or go to the gym all the time, it's not that easy to climb a fence gracefully, let alone quietly. As I pulled myself over I was startled to find that one of the zombies from the house had hold of my shoe. I kicked out and it lost its grip, but the others were lined up and ready for a meal and I only barely got my leg over before they could pull me back down into their yard.

I found myself in some sort of alley, the zombies clawing and hitting the fence in frustration at having lost a meal. The alley seemed clear, but it also looked like it curved around away from the street I needed to get back to.

I jogged hunched over trying to get away from the sounds of my latest escape in case it brought the attention of others. A bit further on the alley opened onto a street with about half a dozen milling about. I pulled myself back into the alley and pulled a protection bubble over myself and ducked behind a prickly bush with less cover than I'd normally like. I was about to add an avoidance layer, but got distracted by the sound of footsteps behind me. What can I say, I panicked.

My body tensed and I just stayed in a squat behind a bush that any normal person would have seen me hiding behind. The zombies on the street seemed oblivious. Suddenly a very mobile group of zombies burst from the alley I'd just come from and into the street. There was pandemonium as the two groups met. The presence and violence of the movements set off the half a dozen zombies already present. They frenzied on the new comers and I tried to move a bit faster toward my destination while they were distracted.

I edged down the block, making sure not to move too quickly or draw too much attention from their new entanglement. I made it to the corner with only half a block to go when I saw JD coming up the street toward me. He was on a motorcycle with some sort of box towed on wheels behind it.

I waved once then crouched down to the ground. With a glance at the street behind me he pulled near the maintenance closet and parked the bike. He grabbed an ax and killed about five zombies making his way to my position. His body was tense and I could tell that he was angry.

"What the hell happened?" He demanded in a whisper. "I was only gone for ten minutes."

"It was longer than that, or it seems like it was. Brad went nuts." I glanced back at the zombie brawl behind us and noted that it had almost diffused. "More nuts, anyway. He ran into the street screaming. I think he was trying to attract those things to the building. We should have tied him up after you knocked him out."

"Crap."

"I think he may have done the same thing to the other survivors in his building." JD gave me a grim look. "Unfortunately you live by the sword and you die by it. He won't be a problem anymore. They ate him."

There was a moment when neither of us spoke. Could we really be glad that he was dead, even with all that he had done? He was after all, one of the last people trying to survive in this hostile new world. A twinge of guilt flexed through me instinctively because I was glad not to be in his company and glad that I hadn't had to make the decision to leave him to die. Difficult times.

I pointed to the new motorcycle he'd acquired. "I was able to move our stuff into that maintenance closet you parked beside." JD turned his attention toward the problem of reaching the cycle.

"Turn radius isn't great on this thing, but if we can get the bags into it and I get enough speed, we can haul ourselves out of town." I nodded. I was more than ready to get the hell out of this city.

JD handed me the ax and we walk-jogged to the maintenance closet. Four zombies came at us, but I held two while I dispatched the others and by the time I was ready for the last two, JD had taken them out with one of the baseball bats in our bags. We switched off weapons and I loaded the backpack and saddle bags in both my hands. JD grabbed the pillow case and the sheet with the stuff we'd gotten from Gloria's and headed for the door, JD in the lead.

I saw a flash of white and black and then JD was on the ground holding the thing away from him. Pus oozed down his clothing as the thing's maw moved in a chewing motion. I dropped the saddle bags and grabbed the ax JD had dropped. I brought it down, but they'd shifted and I only succeeded in creating a wedge between its shoulder and neck. What's worse, the ax wouldn't come out.

Putting my foot on its shoulder and pulling with all my effort it came out, sending me flying and my ass hitting the concrete floor. I scrambled to my feet, ignoring the pain, and brought the ax down again and again. As if in slow motion I could feel the weight of ax as it swung, I saw the things head twist, it's jaws clamp down, JD's jacket-covered arm taking the bite, then the jelly splatter of gore and brain matter.

Chapter 12

JD pushed the thing off him, grabbed his arm and pulled his sleeve up. There were tears in the cloth, small indented scratches on his arm, but not enough to draw blood. He pulled the sleeve down, grabbed the ax from me, heaved the load he was carrying before and hiked toward the bike. I followed in silence, putting a hold on the few zombies that had been attracted to the fight. They stood as frozen as I felt.

We had to shift things around a bit since JD had found a few more guns for our arsenal, but neither of us felt like talking as we strapped the saddle bags on, filled the container attached to the back and climbed onto the bike. We rode out of town directly, no sightseeing, no witty banter or joking around. Things had gotten a little too serious and the weight of that was on our mind.

The indentations, the barely scratched surface of the skin, that wasn't enough, right? You had to be fully bitten, with blood and saliva mixing. That or a scratch, but still, blood and infected tissue had to mix together. It couldn't just be skin contact or an indentation in the skin so light it left little welts. In my mind I went through all the logical arguments why we didn't have to worry, but even through my denial I knew that there might be a possibility. Every time I tried not to think about it, I'd find myself wondering how we could test it, how we could verify JD wasn't infected and how I couldn't lose him now that I'd found him.

By the time we'd returned to the pink Hummer, we were both exhausted from our thoughts. We loaded up and headed back to JD's summer home in complete silence. When we got there he headed into the house without a word, leaving me to bring in our haul. I piled things in the foyer, closed the front door and then set to work sorting things into piles.

When I was done I grabbed all the new clothes, including what looked like a very stylish red plush coat with large brass buttons and deep wide pockets. It was so soft and silky I couldn't help petting it.

"I picked that up for you." I looked up and he was standing there, shirt off, bandage around his arm. He stepped forward and stopped a few feet from me as if afraid of what he might do to me. "The color suits you."

"Thanks." I looked at his bandages. "So, how's the arm?"

"Not sure." He said shifting slightly. "I don't think we ought to take the risk though."

"The risk of what, exactly?" I was starting to get angry.

"The risk of my being infected. I don't want..."
His voice trailed off and he stood up, looking
away from me. "I won't be one of those things.
I won't put anyone else through this."

"You don't even know that you're sick!" I
yelled at him. I grabbed his arm but he pulled
away from me. "Those are indentations, not
scratches, not bites. There is no blood. You're
not sick."

"We can't take that chance." He still wouldn't
look at me. I stepped in front of him and
slapped him so hard my hand stung. He looked
at me then, a wild look that told me just how
panicked he really felt.

"There's a chance for a cure." I pulled the
journal that was wrinkled and bent from the
back of my jeans. "Gloria and this guy, JW,
were working on a cure. We just have to get to
Oregon."

He looked at me and reached for the journal. I
pulled it out of his reach and gave him the
hardest look I could.

"You don't even know who this guy is. Do you
know how big Oregon is or how long it would
take to search for everyone listed in the phone
book with the initials JW? That phone book
may be smaller than San Francisco, but it's still
pretty damn big to go searching for someone
you don't even know and who just as likely is as
dead as everyone else is." My heart lurched and

I just wanted to reach out and hold him, to take away the fear and the despair he was feeling.

"I know his name. It's James Willaker and I think he may be in an area of Oregon that gets a lot of rain." He snorted.

"That's what you've got to go on. That's it?"

"It's a lead, which is better than anything you've got!" I could feel myself on the verge of losing my composure. There had to be a way to fix all of this. Before I knew it I was openly weeping, mostly from frustration, but partly from the fear that all of it was hopeless.

"Are you sure it's Willaker?" I felt JD's hands on my shoulders. I couldn't help it, I was shaking with the need to have a full blown, therapeutic cry.

"Yes. And I also know what the signs are for being infected. I know how it works and if you are infected I won't let you hurt anybody." I turned to look up at him and found him staring at me. "I won't let you give up on me either."

"It's because of your sister, isn't it. That's who you lost." My throat clenched shut and my fingers found the cord around my neck and I pulled the end free, letting the locket dangle for him to see.

"My sister, Sophie." I swallowed hard. I hadn't even said her name aloud since it'd happened and the words felt strange on my tongue.

"You saw her turn?" I nodded, not trusting myself to speak. "You saw her die, didn't you?"

"If you're sick, I'll know it. We have a few days before you show signs, if you're even sick, and we'll just head north into Oregon to find this guy James until we know." He pulled me into his arms and held me, the warmth of his body, the strength in his arms and the beat of his heart pounding in the ear pressed to his chest was very comforting.

"I'm sorry for your loss." My body rocked with sobs and tears pooled and were absorbed by his shirt. We stood there in the foyer, holding each other for I don't know how long.

"I'll get dinner started; the steaks should be thawed by now. Do you want to set the table then we'll discuss this Portland trip you've been talking about." I wiped my eyes and nodded. We walked hand in hand through the house splitting up when we got to the dining room.

I pulled place settings, plates and silverware and arranged them at the chairs we'd sat in before. There were crystal wine glasses that glinted in the light as I set two of them out for us and went in search of the wine cellar. JD directed me to the wine and I pulled a red wine at random from the rack and took it upstairs where I opened it and let it breathe, whatever that means.

By the time dinner was ready, I was in much better spirits. We ate and drank as if there were no cares in the world. We lingered at the table, swapping one-liners, puns and generally having a good time. We were dragging it out until JD started coughing. He gave me a startled look.

"Not a symptom, guy. There's no cold-like symptoms." He nodded but I wasn't sure he was entirely convinced.

"What's this cure you're talking about?" I pulled the journal out and lay it on the table in front of him. He didn't reach for it this time.

"Gloria and a bunch of older wizards were convinced that the plague was begun by magical means rather than by the natural mutation of a virus. That's not to say that it was all magical either." I took another sip of wine. "According to this journal, they found components of a spell that sorcerers and necromancers cast when they are manipulating the dead, but it seems to enhance a naturally occurring virus infection that is normally dormant in most humans. The trick is that if the blood or saliva gets in contact with that dormant virus, it activates and the magic enhances the effects. Voila, zombies."

"So they were trying to track down the sorcerer or necromancer that cast the spell to reverse it, right?"

"They considered that, but logically it doesn't make sense that the person who started it could end it. No one in their right mind would let this go on this long and to such an end. I mean,

162

can't rule the world or whatever if all your subjects are trying to eat you."

"Did they find a counter spell, or whatever?"

"Maybe. See Gloria figured that the necromancer part of the spell could be broken and she had some success with that, but there wasn't really a way to put the virus back to sleep. Also, considering the virus has been in the body as long as it has, the virus has mutated to follow this course regardless. She was working on the spell breaking part and coming up with nothing. Now this guy, James Willaker, was working on a different angle."

"Do tell."

"Initially he thought that the infection and the magic had to be reversed at the same time, but there was some problem with how the two spells worked together to work. According to Gloria, he had some crazy plan to combine three spells, something that's unheard of and monumentally dangerous. She was sure it would fail without some component or link, so she continued to work on it. She thought she might have found something but by then she'd been infected and it wasn't clear that she got whatever it was to James. But she mentions toward the end that as her time was getting shorter, she wished she'd headed north to help him with his experiment sooner."

"How exactly is that a cure?" JD drained his glass and reached for the bottle.

"It's our best shot." I looked at him and waited until his eyes met mine. "It's our only shot at stopping this thing."

"You tried like hell, didn't you?" He returned my look. "You tried and you failed. Again and again and again. You keep telling yourself that you can repair this, make it good again. You can't fix this. You can't fix any of this."

His grip on the bottle was so hard his fingers were turning white, and the grim expression on his face denoted the anger he felt. I reached across the table for the bottle and pulled it from his grip. I swirled the juices in the bottle, watching as the liquid line swayed around and around.

"It's my only shot, finding this guy." I deliberately kept my voice low so he'd have to lean in to hear me. "I'm headed out there with or without you. It'd be safer if both of us went, but if you're going to be a chicken shit coward and piss and moan about how fate has shit in your Wheaties, then stay here. I'll fix it by myself."

With that I pushed myself up from the table, collected my plate and silverware and returned them to the kitchen. I took an alternate route back to the foyer so I wouldn't have to see him sulk. I collected all the books I'd grabbed from Gloria's and marched up to the room I'd stayed in before. I tossed them on the bed, closed the door then returned to the bed to put my fist into a pillow until I'd worked out some of my frustration.

I guess he thought to give me some space because I didn't see him for the rest of the evening. What a crappy way to end the evening. It was an even worse way to say goodbye. Still, he was only looking at the possibility of being infected. So he was determined and caught up in throwing his hands up, which didn't seem like him.

I took a long hot bath, borrowed a robe and did my laundry once I figured out how the damn machine worked. I fell asleep reading spell books in hope of some new revelation. At some point in the night, it seemed like there was someone in the room with me and I started, looking around for the danger. I felt a hand caress my shoulder through the blankets and a low whisper telling me everything was alright. Sleep overcame me and I settled back into the covers.

The next morning I was up and out of bed fully rested. I'd repacked the backpack with clothes and found a duffle for the books. I carried everything downstairs and set my stuff by the door. It was time to say goodbye.

I don't know how I knew I'd find him in the kitchen making breakfast, but it's the first place I checked. Not sure how long I stood there watching him making food in his boxers and a bright white undershirt, but I hoped it would be enough to burn the memory of some good times into my brain. I needed some good times to remember, for the road.

"You just going to stand there or are you going to get your fill before you leave." I stepped forward, opened a cabinet door and pulled out a plate. I held it out while he dished up a ham steak, fresh biscuits and some orange juice. When my plate was full I walked it back to the dining room to eat. JD followed with his own plate.

The awkward silence spread out before us as we sat across from each other. Each movement, each look broadcast our feelings. His of reluctance and shame, mine of resentment and anger. Neither of us brave enough to speak first, but both of us feeling like we'd said what the other needed to hear.

I sat there, babying my juice, trying to make the moment last before I set out on my own. I just wanted him to say something. No, what I really wanted him to do was fight. He was just rolling over and letting this thing happen to him and it made my skin crawl.

With my orange juice gone I stood up. He put his hand out and took my plate and carted it off to the kitchen. I waited for him to return. He stood there, looking at the floor.

"Your best bet is to head up I5 and follow it up. I found the address for Willaker in one of my father's old address books. He's in Portland, a

place that gets more than its fair share of rain.
You might even be able to get the Hummer part
of the way there but don't be afraid to switch
vehicles if things get inconvenient."

"I'll keep that in mind." Icicles dripping from
every word.

"Don't be like that." He spoke softly. "It's not
like I have a choice now. I'm going to become
one of them and I won't hurt you like that.
Watching me die, like you watched your sister
die. Have you watch me become a cannibalistic
freak." He looked up at me, his expression
pleading with me to understand.

"I couldn't be like you," I relied. "I can't just
roll over and take something like this, it's not in
my nature and I didn't think it was in yours
either."

"I'm sick, damn it. Can't you understand that!"
He yelled, his eyes glassy.

"You're not dead yet." I grabbed the keys from
the end of the table where he'd placed them and
stalked out of the room. I couldn't stand to look
at him anymore.

Chapter 13

I grabbed my gear and almost ran out to the Hummer. Throwing my stuff in and slamming into the seat I blinked back the tears. I wiped at my eyes and turned the engine over, the H1 gave a satisfied growl and then I was off.

The signs to I5 were easy to follow once I got back to the main roads. Most of the cars were out of the way, but I had to hop out and push a few of them out of the way. It was slow progress and part of me resented the lack of assistance and companionship. On the plus side there were fewer zombies on the road and in the towns than there were in the city, for which I was relieved. Even the stop for gas was quiet in comparison.

I'd planned on pushing through the night but by Redding I knew that I had to sleep or risk running off the road. I fueled up again, scavenged and cleared out a grocery store and found a mostly empty house off the highway a bit. I cleaned it up, put up some protection and popped a frozen lasagna and frozen garlic bread into the oven. By the time it was done the fire in the fireplace was doing its job at warming up the place.

After cleaning off some dishes I dished out a square and tore off a piece of bread. I'd found an iPod abandoned at one of the gas stations I'd visited earlier and I pushed to let it play. I didn't recognize the band or the song, but my preference in music wasn't an issue. Being alone again was.

Dinner was excellent and I had two servings before I felt bloated and happily full. The bed was a mess, but it was easily solved with a sleeping bag I'd picked up at the last grocery store. I hadn't heard anything moving about and felt too lazy to check the perimeter. Everything seemed ok. I settled in and faded off to sleep listening to some heavy metal band abusing their instruments.

I woke the next morning to an ache in my ears and a scratching sound. I pulled the earphones from my ears and sat up, looking around. Must be some sort of mouse or rat or something. I stood up, straightened my clothes and opened the door to come face to face with milky eyes, grayish skin and a face that had been torn open.

I jumped back and looked around me. If a zombie can be surprised, it was shown only in the two seconds he took to process the situation and lunge toward me. Shit. After jumping back I realized I hadn't thought to bring any weapons into the bedroom with me last night. He stumbled forward again and I jumped on the bed and over it. He fell onto the bed and wrestled with the sleeping bag while I edged around the wall and passed the windows to get to the door. Then all hell broke loose.

The window shattered behind me and I felt the tug of the fabric as another zombie reached through the window, gasping my pants and slicing its arms on the broken glass. I pulled away without being snagged and stepped forward to run for the door when another zombie entered the doorway. It hissed at me through blackened teeth.

Suddenly a bolt shot through its head poking out the left eye. It fell forward and stopped moving. I pulled myself into a corner and saw another crossbow bolt shoot the zombie on the bed. Its struggles with the sleeping bag ceased. I moved cautiously to the doorway and around the wall. JD stood to the side of the fireplace, adding another bolt to the crossbow he was holding.

"Hey babe, looks like you could use some help." He turned the crossbow and without aiming, nailed another zombie in the head with a crossbow bolt. I stepped around the corner watching him as he shot zombie after zombie until there was a small pile of bodies around us.

"What are you—" I cleared my throat. "Did you change your mind, then?"

He walked over, pulled me to him and kissed me, his tongue sliding into my mouth and my body pressing against his with a need I never thought I'd feel again. He ended the kiss and gave me a bemused look. "Thought I might stick around for a while. Heard there was a shot at a cure. Somewhere in Portland, up north."

I hugged him as hard as I could then looked around. Why the hell hadn't my spell worked? Damn it, the spell should have kept them out or at least warned me of their presence. I gathered what was salvageable and packed it in the car while JD stood guard. I saw his motorcycle parked next to the Hummer and saw the heat rolling off it in the morning air. He must've ridden all night to get here.

When I checked the stones I found them where I'd placed them but the magical charge was gone from them. Strange. I gathered the stones together into the pouch and made a mental note to test it later. The magic shouldn't have quit. Unfortunately, there was no one I could ask about it who could tell me what I'd done wrong.

"Take the Hummer," I told JD as he strapped on his helmet. He shook his head and climbed on the motorcycle.

"Better to have options."

I was too relieved to have JD back that I didn't want to mar the morning with an argument. We teamed up to cross the mountain passes into southern Oregon. The cold was getting noticeable and with each pit stop JD pulled his gloves off and rubbed his hands together to warm them. It was getting ridiculous. After one long stretch of curvaceous roads I pulled to the side of the road.

He jogged to the Hummer as I was getting out.

"What's wrong?" I thumbed toward the Hummer and he jumped in the driver seat to check it out. As he was looking at lights and trying to figure out what was going on, I pulled out a pistol and shot each tire, knocking the bike on its side. JD rushed over to me looking genuinely annoyed.

"I assume it offended you somehow." His sarcasm was almost funny if it weren't for the stakes.

"I think it was possessed. We should get in the car and get moving before it comes back." I stepped around him and hopped into the driver seat. He stood for a minute, shaking his head and I'm sure swearing. Then he turned and climbed into the passenger seat and we took off, heater warming us as we travelled.

We drove until we got to Medford, Oregon then stopped for lunch. A couple of sodas and some Hot Pockets later we were ready to set out when JD's arm started bothering him.

"Just itches." He scratched over the bandage.

"Let me see." JD pulled up his sleeve to unravel the bandage and held out his arm to me. There were dark red lines running up his veins and the area where the indentation had been was swollen and red.

"Fuck." He swore under his breath. That about summed it up.

Since it was my turn to drive, I followed the hospital signs up the hill. We had to park at the bottom of the hilly driveway to the hospital because the traffic jam was worse here than trying to go to the mall. The cars were so dense here that we wouldn't have been able to make it even with the motorcycle. I grabbed a gun, he grabbed his crossbow and we loaded as much ammo as we could.

"Why are we stopping here again?" JD asked. "Just out of curiosity, you understand. Or are you just bored and want to kill something?"

"We're here because there may be some way to pull that shit out of your arm. The lines only go part way up your forearm. There has to be some way to suck out poison, from like, snakes or something." I checked the cartridge to make sure I was full then popped it back in. "Besides, I've never heard you complain about killing these things."

He shook his head and we hiked up the hill toward the emergency room.

Chapter 14

There were a few wanderers and we took them out quickly and quietly as we made our way up the hill. The zombies trapped in vehicles that were clawing at the windows, we left. No sense wasting the morning. I kept my eyes looking for threats and not victims. Children especially made me sick. Mothers who'd died giving birth and sat with bowels and stomachs ripped open, the infants devoured, small children struggling against the child seats, clawing at themselves, and the little ones roaming the aisles of cars aimlessly. They were all just so very wrong and I couldn't kill them and I wouldn't let JD kill them.

We made our way to the entrance of the emergency room and found a stack of bodies almost four foot high. People dumped unceremoniously at the doors of the hospital. I took a breath then stepped forward.

The floors were, well, you know all those movies with the blood streaked floors, rubble and body parts, and equipment all over the place and totally deserted? It was like that. There were too many places for zombies to hide and I was starting to have some serious reservations about this.

"Do you know anything about hospitals?" I whispered at JD.

"I've been in one a time or two. Most likely, we need to get into the ER to find what you're talking about. The exam rooms aren't likely to have anything; they don't keep much in there in case some junkie is looking for a needle or a fix."

There seemed to be two ways we could go and one had a double door. I pointed to the doors and JD nodded, crossbow loaded and resting on his shoulder. We moved forward, JD covering the rear. There were no windows, plastic or otherwise in the swinging doors. It was going to be a crapshoot.

I pushed the door experimentally and heard movement on the other side. I stepped back and indicated that he should cover the door. I moved behind him and covered our backs but there was still no movement here. The door moved open and an arm snaked out, pulling itself out to the lobby. JD aimed and waited for the head to peek out before pulling the trigger. It landed with a thunk and he walked over to retrieve the bolt.

He pulled the door open further and peered into the darkened hallway. I backed toward him, trying to see and to cover our backs as he waited for me to catch up. When I caught up to him he whispered in my ear.

"Are you sure you want to do this?" I nodded and he reached into his pocket and pulled out a flashlight no bigger than a sharpie and shone it on the floor. I gagged and stepped out the door to throw up. I wiped my mouth with my hands and resolved to pick up some sanitizer while we were here. When I walked back through the doors he was half way down the hall.

His light shone the path he'd walked, passed severed heads, bodies at all angles and all ages piled on either side of the hall. The center of the hall was a pool of such filth I can't describe. I stepped through it quickly, knowing that I was getting it on my clothes and knowing I would burn them tonight.

We made it to another set of double doors. JD looked at me then pushed it open. A woman stood in the middle of the room, her blonde hair tied up in pigtails and was sitting on one of the ER beds flipping through a magazine. If she was a zombie she was the cleanest and least disgusting zombie I'd ever seen. She looked up at our approach and then at JD who had his crossbow sights on her.

"Hold on there, geez." She put the magazine down on the gurney and blew a bubble with her gum. "Can a zombie do that?"

"Didn't think you were a zombie." JD said, still poised to kill her.

"Oh ho! Look who paid attention in his sorcerer instruction." She turned to me. "Isn't he adorable."

I looked at JD but he didn't move. Sorcerer? I filed the information for a future discussion once we made it back on the road. The woman hopped off the table and walked toward me, the end of the crossbow bolt following her every move.

"But then again, maybe he didn't." She reached her hand out to me. "I'm Sunshine Parker."

"Don't touch her." JD growled. "Casey, back away from her. Now."

I looked from her to him and back, then stepped a few feet closer to the door we'd come in. Sunshine pivoted toward JD, hands on her hips, but with the blonde hair in pig tails and the Nightmare Before Christmas goth look, she just looked like a child imitating what she'd seen her parents do.

"What the hell, man?" She tapped her foot impatiently waiting for an answer, then after a minute of silence. "You think I'm here for you? Or maybe you think that the theatrics with the crossbow would stop me if I were? Put that thing down and play nice."

"What do you mean 'come for you'?" I asked finally. She turned to me and gave me a wide smile opened her mouth to answer, but JD spoke first.

"She's a reaper, Casey. One touch and she pulls your soul out of your body and into the next realm." I noticed a slight tremble to his arms, but it was so slight I wasn't sure if I'd seen it.

"Yeah, but only if you're on my list. Reapers aren't authorized to pull people unless they are about to die. Something about the "natural order" of things." She used air quotations when she said 'natural order'. "Besides, I'm off for a few days." She turned, walked back to where she'd been sitting, hopped back up and watched us.

"A reaper, like, as in death?" She nodded.

"And the crossbow can't hurt you because---"

"I'm already dead, so to speak. I get to keep my body to, you know, blend in, but I get powers and shit." She blew another bubble and popped it.

"So you're a reaper and you have a day off and you are hanging out in a hospital full of dead people and zombies?"

She rolled her eyes. "No, well, sort of. See, I sort of overheard some of the bigwigs upstairs talking about you guys. See the whole zombie thing, totally unexpected. Kinda blew everyone away, ya know? It's not like unexpected shit happens with them so they were freaked out, especially the magnitude of this shit storm."

She looked between me and JD then sighed. "Look, this zombie thing. Unnatural, ok? It wasn't in the big plan that they have. They were whispering about balance being restored and I heard your names. And since there isn't much for me to do anymore, I thought I'd see if I could help."

"How'd you know we'd be coming here?" JD asked adjusting the crossbow.

"Well, thing is—"

"Are we running into an ambush or something?"

"Not exactly, see—"

"Don't screw around with me, reaper."

"I'm not allowed to say directly, but I knew that a questionable medical procedure might be attempted and another somebody might be taking a trip to eternity." I looked at her then at JD. Sunshine looked a bit surprised herself and kept looking up at the ceiling.

"What are you looking at?" I asked trying to see what she was staring at.

"I can't believe they didn't try to pull me. Shit. Things must be really bad if they're not monitoring my every action." She looked at me and the green of her eyes struck me. "You have to get moving; don't stop until you get there."

JD was lowering the crossbow, out of exhaustion or because he believed her wasn't really clear. She turned to him, still sitting on the gurney and smiled.

"Are there any survivors in the hospital?" Not sure what compelled me to ask, but if anyone would know, she would, right?

"Actually, yeah, there are two. Well, one is almost catatonic, but the other one is fully functional. Not sure they'll be much help though." She hopped off the bed and walked toward the door we'd just come in. She turned and waved for us to follow and slipped through the double doors.

I shrugged at JD then started to follow.

"I don't think we should trust her." His face was a bit pale but his eyes were serious. "She's a special kind of trouble. You know what she does. We don't need to be watching our backs all the time."

"So far she's been pretty straight forward, unlike a certain, what was it again? Oh yes, Sorcerer." His eyes turned to the floor. "When were you going to tell me? Why haven't you used your magic? Or were you –"

"My magic is gone." The statement hung in the air. "I bit off more than I could chew and my powers were stolen. I might as well be just any old human."

I stared at him in shock. What the hell did you have to do to screw up and lose your powers? Was that even a thing? From everything I'd read Sorcerers were a bit more powerful because they tended to edge along the darker side of magic if they didn't just dive right into consorting with demons and other dark entities.

"Are you guys coming or what?" Sunshine called out, peeking through the double doors.

I kept my eyes on JD until he looked up at me. The hurt and shame on his face from the admission almost had me reaching out to comfort him. I had to steel myself against it. He hadn't been honest with me and something told me there was more to tell. I gave him a look that suggested this conversation wasn't over, and then walked to the double doors to follow Sunshine.

We followed her through several corridors up to the third floor and then down another maze of hallways. It was amazing how complex hospitals could get. You'd think there would have been zombies around every corner, straining to tear us apart. You'd be right but for some reason they paid no attention to us. At all.

"Is that some sort of spell or something," I asked at one point as Sunshine pushed a slow moving zombie out of the way.

"Like I told you, I got cool magic powers. They're different than yours, of course. Mine have to do with death, the dead, you know, the dying." We walked passed a group of zombies mostly sprawled on the floor gnawing at the air, their blank eyes staring upward at nothing.

"How does it work, I mean, were you a magic user when you were…?" My voice trailed off. She looked at me, and then laughed.

"No, I was just a regular person. Got the powers after I got the job." She turned a corner, and then continued. "There are perks, like, I always get a seat on a plane, no matter how packed and some of my expenses into cool places are taken from the budget."

"Budget? Plane? Don't you just sort of appear and disappear as needed?" JD snorted and I looked back at him. He tried to cover his smile but wasn't doing a good job of it.

"Yeah, see I'm sort of the new kid on the block. I've only been a reaper for about five months or so. You have to get older to do that Houdini shit." She stopped then looked me straight in the eye. "The worst part is that you have to get a freaking day job to support yourself. I mean, you'd think they'd have something set aside for us, but not for the new gal in town. I should have read the contract closer."

"So, wait, if you're dead how do you work?"

"They set you up with a new identity, assign you to an area. If you get compromised, you get a new identity. But thing is they don't provide housing or food—"

"Wait, dead people don't eat."

"The dead, no, they don't eat. Reapers aren't really categorized as being dead. Hence, we have to eat. Not that we can die of starvation but the sensation of starving is still unpleasant until we do eat." She stopped again and turned toward me, her pigtails swaying. "I know this one guy, super old reaper, says he had to cross the ocean for months in a pine box one time getting to a new assigned area. How's that for major suck?"

She grinned and kept going. I was a bit lost and I hoped that JD had been paying more attention to the way out than I had on the way in. My mind was still trying to wrap around the concept of reapers. We walked for a bit and I was so lost in my thoughts that I almost ran into Sunshine when she stopped.

"Ta-da" Her voice rang out. I looked around then saw her helpfully point toward a door. It must be nice to have tracking powers and an anti-zombie aura.

I reached for the handle but JD got to it first. He shouldered me out of the way, gave me a look that said he was taking point then opened the door. The room was dark and the switch on the wall didn't work. JD pulled out his flashlight and swept the room.

"Is anyone in here? I'm not one of them; I'm looking for other survivors. Answer me if you're in here." He crooned into the room, keeping his voice soft and hopefully non-threatening. When he was almost behind the door he stopped suddenly. He looked out the doorway and put his hand up then shut the door.

I couldn't make out the words he was saying, just the timber of his voice. I didn't hear a response, but a moment later he opened the door, a middle-aged woman under his arm. He was directing her out, talking to her, but she looked like she was in some sort of trance.

Sunshine reached out and brushed a lock of hair out of her face. "This is Agnes. She's had a rough time of it. Her group left her here when they stopped for supplies. She just stopped eating, moving, everything."

"Agnes, can you hear me?" I tried to catch her attention, waving my arms in front of her as if she were blind. "Agnes, we're going to take you out of here."

"Do you think that's a good idea?" JD asked, adjusting his grip on her. "I mean, if we're going to be attending to her all the time, it may take away from our main purpose."

"We can't just leave her here." I look around the room at the zombies strewn everywhere.

"Don't you worry." Sunshine piped in. "She isn't damaged in any way that matters. Hey, you might even get her to come out of it."

"All I'm saying is that she'll slow us down. You want her, you take her." JD pushed the woman toward me.

"Fine." I took Agnes' arm and led her to the middle of the hallway. "You said there was another survivor?"

"Come this way!" Sunshine bounced down the hall. "He just got here an hour or so before you did."

I led Agnes and JD followed behind us. We weaved through bodies and hallways. After a few minutes we arrived in what looked like a treatment area. There was a steel cage behind a counter and an out-patient sitting room. In the corner, near the double doors leading out was a shop for glasses and another series of small rooms, probably for flu shots and other quick services provided by the hospital.

There seemed to be no active zombies in the area, and there was the sound of rustling from one of the rooms. I looked at JD. He stood there for a minute then went into the room to check it out while I held onto Agnes. A couple of loud bangs the sounds of scuffling and JD came out holding a man's arm twisted around his back.

"That's Byron." Sunshine whispered to me. "Bit on edge right now, but he's good with a gun."

"Who the hell are you, man?" Byron shouted. JD used the leverage of twisting the man's arms to push him to his knees. Byron yelled in pain and JD released his arm.

"We're here looking for survivors. You fall into that category?" JD sneered at the man. Why couldn't we all just get along?

I gave Agnes to Sunshine who patted the woman's head and directed her to one of the waiting room seats. Byron watched the exchange then looked nervously between JD and myself.

"We're heading up to Portland." I told him. "We have a decent ride and we've been looking for other survivors. We have guns, supplies and of course, transportation. You interested?"

His voice was dripping with sarcasm, "Do I have a choice?"

"Yeah, you do." JD said moving around him. "You want to stay here, you just tell us so and we'll leave. Of course, we may need to secure you before we leave so we know you won't be bothering us."

"JD, what the hell are you doing?" I demanded. "Our fight isn't with this guy or any other people who are still—"

"Human?" JD offered.

"Alive." I finished. Then to Byron I said, "Sorry for the trouble. Just trying to save who we can."

Byron looked at JD with barely concealed distaste as he stood up from the floor. He carefully brushed himself off and walked into the room JD had rousted him out of. When he was gone I looked at JD and shrugged.

"Ok then."

"Crap. I have to go. A bunch of idiots just…"
Sunshine looked at me, then JD. "I'll be back."

She disappeared and I found myself wondering
if she'd ever been there. What a strange
apparition.

"Hope she doesn't." JD muttered.

I reached for Agnes' arm and pulled her to
standing, looked around and we headed out.
We'd have to walk around the hospital a bit, but
it seemed safer than the inside. As we got to the
door we heard a shout.

"Hey, wait for me." Byron jogged over to us.
He held a plastic shopping bag with contents
that clicked as he made his way toward us. "I'm
coming, just needed to get what I came for."

"Yeah, and what's that?" JD asked. Byron shot
him a dirty look.

"None of your damn business, bucko." He
turned to me. "Where's the car?"

I pointed down the hill and he fell in line with
our pace. Agnes stumbled quite a few times, but
she didn't make us carry or drag her through the
wooded areas when we needed to avoid
zombies on our trip back to the car. There was
only one quick stop when we got to the
entrance of the hospital, JD ran in and came out
carrying an emergency kit and a bag of
bandages.

Chapter 15

We got to the car, put our new guests in the back seats and headed north again. We made it as far as Southerlin before twilight set on us. We had to settle for frozen burritos at the gas station we filled up at before we picked a house with quick access to the freeway. We couldn't stay any longer than it took for the sun to provide enough light to see us on our way.

I cleaned the plates and heated the burritos while JD and Byron had a brutal staring contest. Agnes had a staring contest with the wall. Very strange company but much better than being totally alone thinking you may be the last human on earth.

When I brought the food out, everyone except Agnes accepted the plates I handed them. No one ate anything.

"So, Byron is it?" He looked at me out of the side of his eye, determined not to look away from JD first. "What's your story? You travelling around or is Medford your hometown."

He didn't answer for a minute and JD nudged him with his foot. "Lady asked you a question, Byron."

Now Byron wasn't by any means bulky with muscle. He was shorter than me, with a stocky body and a belly that hung over his pants. His hair was graying and he wore wire rim glasses. But what he lack in physique he made up for in persistence.

Byron dove for JD, who was ready for the fight and they rolled around with Byron trying to get a decent hit at JD's face or midsection. Amazingly they avoided dumping the plates of food onto the floor. Since they seemed to be rolling into the other room, I let them get their energy out. Ridiculous as it was I figured in this stress filled environment, everyone needed to have an activity to blow off steam. Besides, I knew JD could handle himself and the situation.

I put the burrito off of Agnes' plate and put it in her hand. To my surprise she lifted it to her mouth and took a bite. Well, that was better than the alternative. If she'd refused to eat we wouldn't have been able to do much for her. None of us had medical experience to work up an IV, let alone take care of her at the basic levels. Hopefully when it came to using the bathroom she'd use the same rote behaviors.

My burritos were still warm and I dug in, occasionally glancing into the other room where the boys were still wrestling. When I was done I got up and went into the kitchen. I found a bucket and filled it with cold water. When I walked into the room where they were still fighting, I pulled the bucket back.

"You don't want to do that, babe." JD said as he held Byron out by his collar. "We'll be done in a minute. We've got a few things more to discuss."

I looked at Byron, his face turning beet red and reluctantly put the bucket of water down. Waste of good water anyway.

Agnes had finished eating and while I waited for the other two to return to their senses, I tried to engage Agnes in conversation.

"Agnes, can you tell me what happened?" She stared out blankly, unmoving. "Agnes, what did you see?"

I jumped as she suddenly became animated.

"They was everywhere," her voice cracked and I got up to get her a glass of water. She sipped it then put it on the floor beside her. She resumed staring at the wall.

"Who was everywhere, Agnes?" I didn't expect an answer, but was again surprised with a response.

"The dead, they was everywhere. We were trapped in one of them big super stores. Plenty of supplies they said, best place to wait for the military to clean things up." She took a shuddering breath. "But some of them we rescued. They were bit, you see. We had no choice."

"What happened Agnes?"

"Was this pretty young thing, close to her time. Her belly so full I'm surprised the baby didn't just jump right out into this world. Not that there was much of a world to jump into. But see, she'd been bit. Oh she was a crying up a storm, begging them to spare her." Agnes looked at me. "Penalty of being bit was to be thrown out to be with your own kind. No half ways about it."

I wasn't so sure I wanted to hear what happened next, but she kept talking.

"They fought about it for quite a while. Finally they figured, if she gave birth we'd keep the baby but throw its mama out the door. Keep her safe by tying her down. No one figured the baby'd try to claw its way out, eat on her from the inside out."

Bile started to rise in the back of my throat. I looked up to see the horrified looks of both JD and Byron. There was no telling how long they'd been standing there but it was long enough. Agnes reached out and started petting the air.

"Hush little baby, don't say a word. Mama's gonna buy you a mocking bird…" She crooned. She started humming the song before breaking into a soft cackle. Agnes pulled her knees up to her chest and rocked back and forth, not saying anything else. She didn't have to.

"Jesus, lady. That's pretty damn sick." Byron said from the corner. He moved to the spot he'd been sitting before and picked up his plate of now cold food.

"How about you?" JD challenged Byron. "What's your story?"

"Whys everyone gotta have a story?" Byron answered, his mouth full of burrito.

"Dude," I said giving him a level look. "There are zombies out there. You'd have to have a story not to have a story, right?"

He thought about it a moment then nodded. "Guess you're right. Not as sick as hers, but I guess it's pretty bad. Any chance we could skip it."

"What do you have to hide?" JD gave Byron a hard stare and he knelt down to retrieve his own food.

"Nah man, just, it's not something I want to remember." His shoulders slumped slightly and he looked toward the other room. "It's painful. I lost my family."

"We all did." I said.

"My wife picked up my kid from kindergarten, been bit by another kid. Not a big deal, right. Except he got sick. My wife was taking care of him and I was going to work, because I had to put food on the table. When we found out about the sickness…" His voice faltered and trailed off.

"We couldn't get a, you know, doctor, to take our calls. Joey was burning up with fever, but just even saying that he'd been bitten and they would hang up on you." He looked at me, the rims of his eyes getting red. "The fuckers hung up."

His accusation hung there, twisting. "My wife, she did what she could but he was delirious. He, he, he didn't know what he was doing when he bit her." Byron began to sob in earnest, great heaving sobs that echoed in the room. JD reached over and patted his shoulder. Byron nodded but kept his face in his hands.

There was nothing to say, we'd all lost something. I patted his shoulder as I walked passed him to the front door. A rickety porch swing was covered in garbage and it took me a few minutes to clear it off so I could sit down. I needed some time to step away from the pain. JD joined me a minute later.

"May I sit?" He asked looking at the opening beside me. I looked at him then back out into the darkness again. He moved around me and sat down.

"Are you going to tell me the rest of your story? Or are you going to lie again?" He sighed and settled back into the chair.

"I knew I ought to have grabbed a pack of beer when we were at the store."

"Did you think it wasn't important? Did you think you couldn't be honest with me?" I stared at him but he didn't meet my eyes.

"I didn't think it would matter." He said plainly. "I lost my powers. I lost everything. If I could go back in time and change that I would, but all this—"

"All what? What happened? And this time you'd better be straight with me."

"I don't want—"

"I don't care what you want." I stood up and kicked the chair.

"I don't want you to hate me for what I've done. And I know that I deserve it, deserve to be hated and cast out, but I…"

"What could be so terrible? Worse than Agnes' story? Worse than Byron's or mine?" I moved in front of him and lifted his chin up so his eyes would meet mine. "Tell me."

"It's my fault all of this happened."

"All of what happened?" He hesitated. "All of what?" I repeated.

He pulled his chin away and motioned for me to sit down. I didn't want to give him the upper hand but it seemed like I was closer to the truth. That's all I wanted, I told myself.

"I was conjuring a demon, but I forgot part of the spell in my haste to prove that I could do it. I made a rookie mistake." He ran his hands through his hair. "The demon came at my call and it knew, it knew I'd forgotten part of the spell, but it didn't let on."

"That's how you lost your powers?" He nodded and I nudged him to continue.

"It tricked me. I wasn't careful enough in my words or with my spell and it got the upper hand. I lost control."

"So, it got the upper hand. What did it do?" He opened his arms and held them out for a moment, then dropped them.

"Wait. You're saying the demon you conjured created the infection?" He nodded.

"Not only that. It's worse. It stole my powers and used them to create the infection, to activate it and to spread it." Silence fell between us as his words sank in.

"Why didn't you take care of it then?" I wanted to yell but kept it low making my throat feel strained. "Didn't you have some sort of backup plan?"

"Did you miss the part where I lost my powers? And I knew I'd made a terrible mistake as soon as it had taken my powers, but I couldn't do a damn thing about it. Why do you think I've been searching around for someone…?"

"Someone with magic to clean up the mess." I finished for him. We sat in silence for a few minutes then he stood up and went back inside without a word.

I sat on the porch swing all night, my mind numb from all of it. All the pain, all the misery, all of it because a spell hadn't been correctly cast. It didn't make a difference that it was JD, it could have been me and I would have felt the same. To have to live with that, to see all of this and know what we knew and experienced what we'd done.

Chapter 16

The sun rose in the sky a pink and golden light cast over everything. I stood up, my feet numb to the point of pins and needles as I applied the pressure of standing on them. Flexing and stretching helped. I took my time and made my way inside.

Agnes was curled up, sleeping on the floor where she'd eaten. Byron was on the couch in the other room. I slipped quietly passed them looking for JD. He wasn't in either of the bedrooms, the bathroom or the kitchen. I walked out the back door and saw him sitting on a boulder off to the side. He looked like a lost little boy, sitting on a rock, waiting for somebody to come back for him.

My approach was quiet, but not silent enough.

"Go away." His voice was gruff. "I'm not interested."

I circled the boulder and pulled myself up. As soon as I got to the top he lunged at me, pushing me back. I fell with a thud onto the dirt and rocks below. The wind knocked out of me, I lay there for a minute. I stood up, dusted myself off, and began climbing again.

"I said go away!" He lunged again, but I was ready for him this time. I grabbed his foot and dropped my weight, pulling him down to the earth with me.

Before I could react he flipped over and pinned my arms above me, his legs on either side of my body. His breath was warm and came in quick gasps against my neck.

"I don't need this. And I don't need you." I just lay there looking at him. "Take your friends and get out of here. Now."

"No." He picked up my hands and slammed them against the ground. I took in the pain but didn't call out. I was in some sort of strange calm. Baring his teeth he put his face into mine and yelled.

"What the hell are you doing, man?" Byron stood by the backdoor with the look of someone who has been roused out of a deep sleep.

"Get back inside." I yelled. "Everything is fine."

Byron looked like he doubted that but he turned and walked back in the house, closing the back door.

"Is it fine, Casey? Is it really?" JD released my hands and I pulled them to my chest, rubbing my wrists. "Is everything going to be all right? This is just a bad dream that we'll all wake up from."

He stood up and grabbed a rock and threw it into the tree line, then kicked the boulder.

"You know, I've gone over it in my mind. What happened, what I could have done, what I should have done. And you know what it comes down to? I did this. I did all of this."

"JD—"

"No," he cut me off. "Don't even try to suggest that it's not my fault. I know it is. Don't try to convince me that it will be ok, because I won't believe you."

"I wasn't going to." I rolled up to a sitting position. "I was going to say, man up. We have to get moving if we're going to find a way to fix this thing."

"Man up? That's all you've got is…" It looked like he couldn't decide which way to go. To hit the tree, to shake some sense into me, to scream. All good choices, I suppose. I stood up.

"Ok, you fucked up. You fucked up in a major, mind-blowing, world ending way. Does that change the fact that we have to get to Portland to fix it?" I couldn't interpret the expression on his face. I'd say it was awe mixed with WTF and are-you-insane?

"Now if you're done with this pity party nonsense, get your ass in gear and let's get going. The sooner begun, the sooner done." I waited. Like the confusion in what to do earlier, he couldn't seem to focus on what to say in response. In the end he looked at the ground, nodded, then looked me in the eye before he walked back into the house.

We didn't have much to load in the car because we'd left most of it out there all night. Soon we were making more progress on the way north, taking turns pushing cars out of the way. With the exception of Agnes, we managed a few decent conversations that almost seemed like a normal road trip. Still everyone was more subdued than the previous day.

JD's mood I could understand and, well, Agnes was Agnes, but Byron was a little distant. Every time anyone got close or too personal he'd shut down. The manners that'd been drilled into me by my mother suggested that he'd had a hard time and was mourning his personal loss or was reluctant to relive any memories of the ones he'd lost, but the curious part of me wondered if there wasn't something more.

We stopped for gas and everyone split up. Byron took a turn at the pump, Agnes stayed in the car, JD went to raid the snack and soda machines and I went to stretch my legs.

I walked up the mound of dirt and crab grass to look at the line of trees and emptiness ahead of us. It was amazing that we'd made it this far. I heard pebbles skitter behind me and waited for company.

"Hey, we should be getting back. We've got a ways to go yet today." I took his hand in mine and squeezed it.

"Do you think I can do it?" I whispered pulling the journal out of the back of my pants where I now kept it.

"If not you, then there's no one else." He sighed. "I've looked. Believe you me."

"What if I make things worse? What if—"

"What if you screw up like I did?" He squeezed my fingers and let go. "Can't screw up the world much more than it already has been. Besides, I'll be there with you. I won't let you screw up."

It shouldn't have made me feel better, but it did. I smiled and turned to him. Then I yelled.

My hot pink Hummer was making its way back onto the freeway.

"What the hell is he doing?" I screamed, but JD was already running to cut them off. I've never seen anyone run so fast as I saw him flying down the mound of dirt and vaulting, with abandon, the debris. To his credit he made it in time to slam into the side of the H1 and fall back on his ass before it jumped the side and drove north without us.

It took me a few minutes to catch up with him and only because he was walking to meet me.

"Was that Byron or Agnes?" JD gave me a dark look then grabbed my arm and held me there while he looked around.

"Agnes isn't capable of tying her own shoes, let alone driving. Byron's not right in the head." He started walking north the direction the Hummer was headed. "He was loading up on needles and drugs when I found him in that room. He's an addict. Don't know what he thinks he's doing, survival maybe."

"Oh god, all our guns and all our…" My voice trailed off.

"We just need to find a vehicle and we can push on." I looked around and couldn't see a single vehicle that looked serviceable.

"What about at the gas station? Maybe a car we didn't see somewhere." JD shook his head.

"We may be walking for a bit." I looked at his arm and the dark veins had spread passed the bandage. Walking would only push the infection that much faster. Besides, we needed to get there now.

"We don't have time for this."

"We can't do anything else. Unless you have a better plan? Let's go."

We walked for a couple of hours before we made it into one of the smaller towns along the highway. There wasn't much to choose from and JD was starting to look a little pale. We ended up hot wiring a Subaru Outback and popping some gardening gear and a shotgun with no ammo.

I insisted on driving while JD slept. To make up the time we would have to drive most of the night. We made it into a town with a Walmart where it took eight zombies to get into the WalMart, two dozen zombies to find what I needed and another four to get back to the car.

We laid the back seats down and put a couple of sleeping bags in the back with camping pillows. I'd managed to salvage a first aid kit and we'd re-bandaged his arm for what it was worth. His temperature was going up but he didn't have the majority of the symptoms yet. It didn't stop him from trying to work out a promise that I'd leave him by the side of the road when it became clear that he was going to turn.

I evaded again and again, but as the time went on he started getting weaker. I stopped waking him when I needed to move a car. I took out the zombies on my own with baseball bats and a gardening hoe. We made it up to Eugene before the fever started to rise to dangerous levels.

Chapter 17

"Let me out somewhere along here." I heard a voice from the back of the car. I hit the gas a bit harder and rammed a police motorcycle off the road a bit further. I put it in reverse and drove through the expanded opening.

"You can't just ignore this. And you can't ignore me forever." I kept my eyes forward, watching the road and trying to guess which side would be more open to passing. This area was a bit thicker than the longer stretches of road.

"At least stop for the night," he begged. "You're exhausted and you need to rest."

I let his voice roll over me, as if I had the radio on. I wasn't going to stop, not until I'd found a way to save him and everyone else left in the world.

He finally gave up or succumbed to the fever that was getting worse by the hour. I pushed through Eugene traffic, fueled up and hit the gas to make it to Salem before the sun rose again. My eye lids felt like wet leather, heavy and not part of my body. My head fluffy and light, my concentration was next to nothing. When I ran us off the road into a field of tall yellowish white plants, I knew that I had to stop for a rest.

With protest from the back I managed to get us onto a dirt trail that allowed access to the fields which led up to a quaint farmhouse. I cleared the dead bodies and helped JD into one of the bedrooms. It looked like it was home to a boy with much love for football.

"I don't want to do this, but—"

"Please, just do it."

I cast the spell around him that I'd cast around my sister, restricting him to the bed. There was a bucket with toilet paper rolls for a bathroom. While I still intended to save him, he was right that I couldn't take the chance. It didn't help that he was so damned insistent on being locked up and treated like one of those things.

Looking at him as he sunk onto the bed clearly as exhausted as I was, I just wanted to go back to that night in his summer house. Maybe just to hold him again. To kiss those lips. I walked into the other bedroom and dropped into a deep sleep.

"Casey, you don't have much further to go."

I was standing by the bay again.

"What is it about the bay, Sophie, that you keep coming back to this particular moment."

She turned and smiled at me, not answering.

"Fine. Be mysterious, just tell me how to fix all this. I found the journal, I'm on my way north to Portland."

She reached back for my hand. I paused before stepping forward between the rocks and taking her hand in mine.

"Have you ever wondered what you would do if you could do it all again?" She asked looking at me, her eyes as blue as mine and our dark hair dancing in the breeze.

"You can't do it all again, Soph, that's impossible."

"What if it was? What would you do differently?" I thought for a moment. I could get to JD faster, we could go straight for the cure without him getting infected. Maybe even just come straight to Portland and save hundreds of thousands of people. I looked at her and a flash of dark flitted behind her eyes.

"Who are you?" I demanded trying to free my hand. "What have you done with Sophie?"

A dark, gravely voice spoke from my sister's lips.

"Your Sophia is mine. They all are. And I don't give up what is mine." I pulled in earnest, tugging to get away from the iron grip she had.

"I'll stop you!" I shouted. "I'll save them all and I will destroy you. Destroy you for everything you've done."

It just laughed and the chills ran up my spine. I'd guessed correctly. I moved toward the water, pushing toward the vortex in the water, but the thing disguised as Sophie continued to hold my hand as we were both sucked closer to the center. It gave me an evil grin as the clawed hands tore into us.

I woke in a cold sweat, breathing heavy. From the light coming in from the window I couldn't tell if it was dawn or twilight. I checked the freezer and found some frozen beef and a Hungry Man dinner. I chose the Hungry Man and popped it into the microwave. Eat first, then bring back dinner for JD.

While the food was cooking I checked in on him. He was curled up in the tiny bed, the sheets looked damp and I could feel the heat coming off him from three feet away. He didn't have much time. Maybe not even time to eat before we hit the road.

My stomach growled, low and angry. "You sound hungry. Eat something before you go."

"I'm not leaving you." He whimpered and all I wanted to do was reach out and comfort him.

"You have to leave me. I won't be able to control myself when I become one of them. Don't make me die knowing that you're going to do the dumb thing."

"You said you'd be there with me, when I did this. You gave me your word you lying bastard."

He gave a weak cough and cleared his throat which spurred a coughing fit that sounded wet and sticky. I knew the signs, I knew the symptoms. Sophie. Now, JD. As much as I wanted him with me, I knew that he was right. He wouldn't be going any further than this farm house.

"We'll all be there with you, Casey. You'll take our strength and our spirit with you." Another cough that sounded like he was choking, but he managed to clear his throat. "Casey, every last person will be there with you. You won't be alone."

The microwave beeped and he laughed but it sounded like a snort. I didn't want to leave him like this, but I turned back into the kitchen and pulled out the meal I'd prepared. I needed my strength if I was going to fight this, and fight I would.

Chapter 18

Before I left I offered to move him into the bedroom I'd slept in, but he declined. He was too weak to move, he said, and it was more of a danger to me to try to help him into it. He didn't point out that as a zombie you didn't care about the accommodations.

I'd never felt more wretched or alone as the last several hundred miles into Portland. But as wretched as I was, the anger and fury was building. I'd lost everyone and everything I'd ever had. My sister, JD, all those innocent people, civilization, all of it. Clean showers, easy travel, the security of walking down the street without looking over your shoulder. Even my life seemed insignificant in light of all that had been taken.

Checking the address from a map of Portland, it looked like Mr. Willaker was in Lake Oswego, just south of the city of Portland. Even better. The outskirts of the city would be safer with fewer corpses to put down. Yeah, I was in the mood to kick a little ass.

Traffic was easier than I'd imagined. It looked like someone had come this way at some point and I could discount the idea that there might be more survivors this way. Cars and debris seemed to be pushed to the side and I swear the tire tracks off road at times looked like those of a Hummer. If I ran into Byron, his ass was grass too for leaving us to die out there.

According to my map, there were streets that seemed to ring around a lake which sat at the center. Looking at it, it looked more like a pond. I drove toward the street name I was looking for and followed the numbers.

For some reason I was surprised to see the pink H1 parked in front of a two story house with columns on either side of the front door. I checked the address and the house number, it was a match. But why would Byron come here? How had he known about James Willaker? There was only one way to find out.

I parked the Outback behind the Hummer and got out. As I walked to the door, I kept my eye on the neighborhood. It looked like it had been cleared out of bodies, moving or not. If I hadn't been so angry I might've peeked in the windows, but I didn't have any weapons with me other than my magic. Hopefully that would be enough.

As I approached the door, I could feel that something wasn't right. The world, in general, hadn't been right in a while, but this was different. It felt like a loaded gun, just the sheer potential pushing the outer edges of this time and space. Maybe it was just nerves. Maybe it was a spell. Or maybe I'd found James Willaker.

As I approached the front door I noticed it was open a crack and not firmly closed. I wouldn't have to worry about the lock. It didn't take much and the door swung open. A momentary musing and I found myself smiling at the thought that JD would have kicked the door in anyway. He seemed like that.

Inside the floors were hardwood cherry and the foyer was short, with a sitting room both to the left and right. The foyer extended to a hallway that looked like it entered into a kitchen. I stepped inside, sobered by the task at hand, and looked for signs of life.

The house was dark and my eyes took a moment to adjust. Some light came in through the bay windows that opened up each sitting room. There didn't seem to be anyone here, but I was certain with the pink Hummer parked outside that Byron and Agnes wouldn't have left it behind. I guessed it was a living room on one side and a sitting room on the other, but I'd never really understood the difference. I guess I just didn't fall into that tax bracket.

Both rooms were trashed and hastily put back together. Pillows were askew and there were a few bits of ceramic from a damaged lamp as if someone had thrown it across the room. Strange.

I centered myself, closed my eyes and pulled my will into a searching spell. I was looking for what was hidden. I needed to search the entire house, but it would be easier to know where I was going than to move from room to room. The house had already been searched, it may already be too late, but that wasn't going to stop me from trying. If James was half as crafty as Gloria, he wouldn't have made the knowledge so easy as to be found by tossing pillows and throwing vases. Besides, if Byron and Agnes were still here, they'd be hiding and I would have a chance at knowing where they were so I could deal with them.

My spell built up quickly, but enlarging it took effort and concentration. I moved against a wall in one of the sitting rooms so I could have some chance of defending myself. A headache twinged at my temples with the effort of pushing magic into such a large endeavor. I pushed on the outer edges and felt tendrils exploring the edges of my spell. There was something hidden in the sitting room I was standing in, something that didn't feel right, but it wasn't quite what I was looking for. I kept searching.

"Look who's here." Byron's voice floated to me. My concentration wavered and I dropped the spell. "We've been waiting for you."

He stood with shotgun leaning against his shoulder. I didn't move, I just watched to see what he would do. There was a part of my brain that wasn't quite sure what was going on. I mean, Byron may have been an addict or something, but why come here? Why now?

"Where is he?" Byron demanded. I shrugged. He pulled the shotgun from his shoulder and aimed it at me. "Where is he?"

"He's checking the perimeter." I moved my head toward the window. "Should be here any minute."

He hooted in laughter. "You're a lying bitch. You're not even that good of a liar." He motioned me to start moving in the direction of the kitchen with the end of the gun. "I was watching you come up the street. Saw you get out. He ain't with you."

"Then why'd you ask?" I wanted to keep him talking to see if I could figure out what his game was.

"I want to know where the bastard is. Now you tell me or we're going to go upstairs and have ourselves some fun." He gave me the full body scan with his eyes and I wondered if I'd ever feel clean again.

"He got bit and had to stay behind. No thanks to you, asshole." His look darkened and he lifted the gun to his shoulder long enough to step forward, grab a handful of my sweatshirt and toss me into the sitting room I'd sensed something a bit off. As I rolled I felt magic. It was as if I'd been gently patted down, caressed even. Something important was here.

"Take off your top." I glared at him, not moving. I didn't need to speak to recall my spell, but I did need to concentrate. Byron might not give me the time I needed. I concentrated my searching spell, trying to pinpoint the sensation I'd felt. It seemed to be, wait that couldn't be right, but it seemed to be reaching out to meet my searching spell.

"I said take off your top or you ain't going to have a top to take off." He emphasized the threat by cocking the gun and pointing it at my chest. I pulled the sweatshirt over my head, leaving my t-shirt on.

"Mmm mmm, much better. Aren't you more comfortable now? Now let's see what you got under that shirt." My fear and loathing must have increased my concentration because my spell did something I'd never seen it do before. Near the fireplace I could see the glowing outline of a pulpit with a sheaf of papers sitting on it. That was it, that was what I was looking for.

I pulled my t-shirt over my head, revealing a lacy red bra and my bare skin. He made appreciative sounds and rubbed himself with his free hand. Somewhere inside, past the humiliation and the survival necessity, I determined that this sicko would pay. If I had anything to say about it, I'd be involved.

His eyes glazed and I could see this was going to escalate. I dropped my searching spell and readied something that would be a little more shocking. I smiled.

"You like that too, huh? I got more to offer you than that asshole ex-boyfriend of yours." He laughed. "Especially now."

I moved toward him and lifted my hand, casting as I moved and forcing the electricity toward my hand. He really didn't know what hit him. He flew backward, crashing over furniture and landing in a heap on the floor. I snatched my t-shirt and slammed it over my head.

"Sure you want a piece of me?" I called to him as I pulled the sweatshirt over my head. Oh no, I wasn't through with him quite yet.

"Where's Agnes? What did you do with her?" I stepped into the living room but this crumpled form was gone. I started to look behind me but dove for the floor when I heard the click. The sofa exploded into foam and chunks of plywood.

I scrambled to the end of the couch and threw a holding spell in the direction I thought he might be standing. As it was my aim was off because I only caught half of him and it was just my luck that I caught the half without the gun.

A muffled cry and the couch exploded where I'd been crouched. I threw another lightening spell over my shoulder hugged the floor. I smelled the acrid smoke before I saw it. I peeked through the shambles the couch had become and saw the wall singed and smoking. No Byron though.

If I moved quickly I could get the pages I needed from James's pulpit, I could stop all of this. I moved as silently as I could toward the foyer. No one was there or in the hallway. I was moving across into the sitting room when I heard a sharp, loud scream. It was coming from upstairs.

Agnes.

Chapter 19

I looked up the hallway and from my new angle I could see the handrails to the staircase going up. There was no time to decide, but I hoped like hell I'd have time to get up there to help her. I ran toward the stairs next to the kitchen.

"What the hell are you doing Byron?" I screamed as I reached the top.

Byron stood there, knife dripping with blood, Agnes' head held over what looked like a summoning circle drawn on the floor and a thin line on her cheek that oozed blood. I looked at Agnes. Her eyes were wildly rolling back and forth and her breath was coming in short gasps. Her hands and feet had been bound with duct tape, probably the stuff I had in the Hummer, and now she was at the mercy of this psycho. The angle that he held her head up from the rest of her body must have made it difficult to breathe.

"You can't stop it now, bitch." He was baring his teeth at me, his skin red and blistering, with patches of hair missing from where I'd shot him with lightning. "I'm going back, and I'll make sure my family is safe from those things."

"What are you talking about?" I slid my foot forward to step into the room but he pulled the knife closer to her throat, drops of blood spotted the floor. "How are you going to go back?"

"He promised me." A sick giggle escaped his lips. "He promised me that if I could stall you or get you here to find the treasure that he'd send me back. Back to when my son was bit, back before my wife was infected, back before all of this."

"Who told you this?" I lowered my voice, slowed the tempo. I needed him to stay calm because if he pulled that knife any closer, Agnes might not make it. "Who said they could take us back?"

"Not us. Bitch!" He pulled the knife from her throat to point it at me. "Not you. You're to be the second sacrifice to ensure that my family survives!"

I pushed my will into a holding spell but he'd already begun pushing the knife into Agnes' throat. Things slowed to the point where it seemed like I was moving through molasses, thoughts floating to the surface, wondering whether I'd be able to stop him and knowing that it was too late. Things switched from slow motion to sonic speeds the instant the artery opened.

Arterial spray and a flooding pool of blood spread over the summoning circle. Byron frozen in place and I could see, even in the low light, the life spark of Agnes' eyes going out.

"What the hell?" I heard a woman's voice behind me. I turned to see Sunshine standing there, holding a notecard in her hand. "What the hell happened?"

I couldn't find the words to explain so I turned back to look at the scene. A small trail of smoke was rising from the center of the summoning circle, curling in and around, and then spreading upward. It coiled and weaved, getting thicker, stronger until it became tangible.

"What the hell? Oh shit." Sunshine said and I agreed. What the hell, indeed.

Byron threw himself on his knees and raised his hands toward the figure emerging from the dark smoke. He was laughing and crying and soaking up Agnes' blood with his pants. Agnes' body was still of even death spasms; she was gone.

"My lord, my savior," cried Byron, who was now trying to bow over Agnes' sprawled form. "I have done as you have asked; I have sacrificed this woman in your honor. Please, I beg of you as your servant, fulfill your promise and send me back through time to my family, to save them from this cursed infection."

"Now, now, we must have patience." A timbered voice floated around the room. "There will be plenty of time for that once we see what we have here. Once we see which of my tasks you have successfully completed."

I felt a breeze blow passed me, but something about it made a shiver run up my spine. I turned to Sunshine who had stepped back and mouthed 'I'm sorry I didn't know' to me across the hallway. I turned back and watched as the smoke and shadows tightened their form into the shape and body of a man in his thirties.

He was blonde with a chiseled chin and Ken doll eyes. If you didn't know that he was a demon, he'd be the prettiest boy in the room. God and luck save you if you went off to some dark corner to get to know him better. And may they save you again if you survived to come away from the encounter. Demons were bad business, to be avoided when possible.

"Well, you are a pretty little thing to be causing so much trouble." He said, appraising me from head to toe. I could feel a sort of magic pressing in on me, assessing my strengths and my weaknesses.

"So you're the one I've heard so much about." I said, trying to keep my voice cool and collected. No sense letting him know that every fiber of my body was screaming to get the hell out of there. He probably already knew anyway. "You've caused quite a stir."

He laughed and it was so inviting that I found myself straining to keep from wanting to entertain him and be in his good graces. I couldn't let the seduction win. Everyone has a darker side and demons play on that, the trick is to know that darker side and to have a firm lid on it. Fortunately, I spent more than a few years looking into mine.

"And what exactly have you heard." He paused to kick Agnes' body a foot toward the outer edge of the summoning circle. "About me."

"You tricked a sorcerer and stole his powers." He gave me a smile and lifted his hands in a gesture that said 'what else could I do?'

"It's in my nature. What else have you heard?" I avoided looking into his eyes when I answered.

"That you're making promises about going back in time." I looked meaningfully at Byron who was still on his knees bowed so far forward his forehead touched the blood soaked carpet.

"Ah yes, that." He raised an eyebrow at me. "Are you interested?"

'Yeah, right.' I thought. 'For a one time price of your immortal soul.'

He seemed to hear my thoughts and replied, "Of course, no soul is required for this transaction. I'm perfectly willing to give you the same deal I gave Mr. Parser here."

We both looked at Byron and sensing our attention he sat up on his knees. Upon seeing the demon Ken doll, he began to weep and beg again for the reward that was due him. I guess the demon, tired of his devoted servant, decided to get him out of the way because an inky blackness swirled from his out stretched finger.

The blackness was a type of magic I'd never seen before. It looked almost liquid in consistency and the way the light was absorbed into it, well, it was hypnotic to watch. Suddenly it lashed out, spiking Byron through the center of his forehead. Byran shot back, ramrod straight back into the most uncomfortable position I'd seen a human body contort. His face was pale and beaded with sweat, his expression one of horror.

"That ought to keep him busy for a bit, don't you think?" I looked away. "Now, now, I'm not going to leave him here. He'll go back in time with the rest of you. He's just getting a little reminder of what he's been through so he knows what he needs to do in his second chance."

"I never agreed to your deal, demon."

"Yes, of course you haven't, but you will." He stepped a few feet closer and I scooted back to the railing at the top of the stairs. "You see, I know all about you, Casey Danvers. I know that you lost your sister to this, ah, ugliness."

He stepped out of the summoning circle and through the doorway. "Your poor, poor sister. Yes, Sophia is mine, as are all the others. But you can change that. Just think."

His hand reached out suddenly toward my head and I flinched. But he very gingerly pushed a lock of hair out of my face and over my ear. I kept my eyes down.

"If you had known then, what you know now." He chuckled. "You could make different choices Casey. You could save the people you have come to care about."

"Save them?" I said, still keeping a rein on my terror level. "How could I save them?"

"Well, maybe not all of them. But some." His brow wrinkled. "You know, save the ones you really care about."

"And leave the others to die?" I asked. "To watch things degrade as they have before? To make new mistakes and lose more people to this, this, plague."

He rocked back on his heels for a moment and said nothing.

"I'm offering you a chance to save your sister." He said, his voice growing ominous.

"At what price, though." My voice had more of a challenge than I intended.

"Nothing much, Casey. All I need is for you to find the spell I'm looking for and I'll give you your sister back. I'll give you JD back. You can try again."

To see Sophia alive again. To hold JD in my arms once more. Images, memories flashed through my brain. Times I'd spent with both of them. The love pulsed through me and I was tempted. I was so damn tempted. My chest felt like it'd been hit hard with the longing I felt just to see them alive again. It was all I really wanted. And then suddenly the images changed.

The image of Sophia remained but her eyes were dripping with blood, her nails extended into talons and her flesh peeled off her in chunks. My mind rebelled against the sight, the thought of Sophia like that. I heard a scream, but it wasn't in my mind; it came from behind me.

"That's quite enough from you, Reaper." The demon waved his hand and Sunshine was gone. "We should retire downstairs, have some tea and discuss this."

"What did you do to her?" I asked, my voice wavering slightly.

"Oh, nothing terrible. Let's just say she'll be occupied for a little while." He extended his hand to me. When I didn't take it, he added, "Reapers can't really die, but they can be put in their, ah, places."

I glanced at his face and he smiled, the edges of his eyes crinkling slightly. Ignoring the hand I swung around the edge of the banister and made my way down the stairs. As I walked, I was thinking furiously about what my options were here. After seeing his magic, it made mine look like an amateur magician. This thing not only had dark powers, but JD's magic to boost them. I couldn't be sure that my spells would be strong enough. I was certain that I'd only get one chance when the time came, if it ever did, so it better be done right.

"Please, take a seat in the sitting room, if you would. I'll get the tea."

Chapter 20

As I walked toward the hall thoughts of making a run for it ended as the front door slammed shut and locks flew in place. I walked slowly, trying to decide between options for fighting and escape and coming up with a rather short list. By the time I reached the space between the two rooms I was so distracted that I was surprised to see the podium still standing there. But more than that, there was now a glowing ring on the carpet, woven, somehow, into the pattern of vines in the rug.

It was ingenious. I looked up to see if the demon was watching or noticing my attentions, it wasn't. If there was anything that could stop all this, it was there at that podium. I heard the rattle of cups on saucers and jogged to the room opposite of the one with the podium.

The demon came down the hall, looked right then left and smiled when it saw me.

"I said we should try the sitting room, this would be the living room."

I shrugged. "Never really familiar with the difference. They're really the same thing with different names as far as I'm concerned." It gave me a polite smile that told me that it didn't agree, but it set down the tray with tea on the coffee table in front of me.

"Have you had a chance to find the spell I'm interested in, my dear." Its tone was mild but there was a self-satisfied tinge to its words as if I'd played into its trap.

"We can discuss that once the terms are agreeable," I said, looking at the tea warily. Normally I wouldn't trust a demon, but would it kill me before it had what it wanted? It needed that spell.

As I was looking between the available cups it occurred to me how strange the request was. Why would this thing need the spell if it was going to roll back time? Rolling back time would move things back for everybody, including the wizard who created the spell. So why... oh.

"Would you like lemon or sugar with your tea, Casey?" It was being awfully civilized.

"This rolling back of time," I began, "Would I go back to exactly where I was or where I wanted?"

Its humanly soft, breathy chuckle felt like satin in my ears. Still, I resisted. No better than a good late night DJ, I told myself. I will not be seduced by this thing.

"Are we negotiating then?" It picked up one of the cups of tea and seeing that I hadn't picked up mine asked, "My dear, I'm sorry. Did you want this one? Less likely to be poisoned or something of that nature?"

I gave him a level look and sat back on the couch with my arms folded. It shook its head and settled into the other end of the couch, sipping its tea softly. It gave a contented sigh and then turned its attention on me again.

"I would need to see the spell before I could even begin to negotiate the where and the when." It lowered its head and looked up at me while batting its eyes. When I didn't respond, it continued, "I assume you want to get to the time and place where your sister was bit by one of those nasty, horrid creatures."

I nodded, not wanting to give myself away by speaking.

"That's very clever of you. Unfortunately Mr. Parser didn't think that far, ahem, pardon the pun, but didn't think that far ahead." The demon chuckled lightly as it sipped its tea. It seemed that Byron would be reliving his family's infection and death again. Wording was everything in these negotiations.

If I could get him to roll back time, but allow me to be near Portland I could keep James Willaker alive. Call me cynical, but if I found out there was a major hole in my plan, I'd want a second chance to make sure that hole never got made. But why did he need to see the spell, I wondered. Why not roll back time now and correct its mistake. There was something that I was missing.

"If you'll produce the spell, we can begin negotiating in earnest." It patted my knee. "I'll even promise to abide by the spirit of your requests instead of the typical demon-thing of twisting it around on you." He rolled his blue eyes and smiled as if we were sharing a little secret.

"I'm not going to be able to do that," I said, standing up. I found myself slammed into the couch so hard the wood beneath me snapped and my body reeled from the sudden pain.

"And I'm just as sure that you will be able to do as I ask," It said mildly. "I don't see that you have a choice. You see, your sister's soul does hang in the balance. I can make things very, very simple for you. Or I can make them very, very traumatic."

I couldn't move to push myself up, couldn't breathe from the pressure of being held down. My body screamed for air and freedom and I could provide it neither. Just when I thought I might black out, the pressure eased up. I was still stuck on the couch, but I could breathe and move my arms at least.

I glared at the demon. "Now, now. We had to get that out of the way. You need to know that we won't be leaving here without an amenable conclusion to this negotiation. And it will go much smoother if you were reasonable and polite about the whole thing. No need to make it uglier than it already is."

"What if I refuse your offer?" I asked. "What if you have nothing to offer that would interest me? What then, demon?"

"Oh please, call me Rick." It put the cup into its saucer and placed it gently back onto the tea tray. "I'm sure we can find something that you want. If not your sister, then perhaps someone else. Maybe that nice young man you were travelling with. What's his name? Ah yes, JD."

I could feel the magic working this time, the magic invading my mind, my memories. Images flashed through my mind, but I held tight to my reservations. This desire and longing could be refused. It could be rebutted. I pushed my consciousness into a ball and held tight until the display was over.

We sat in silence for a few minutes. The demon licked its lips in anticipation of my agreement. When my eyes cleared and I could see the world as it was again, I released my conscious mind and shook my head. The demon frowned and looked down at the carpet.

"Oh dear," it said. "I was hoping that we could do this in a civilized manner."

A flash seared through me, and all I could see was white, hot pain. My bones felt rubber, my blood boiled and my skin crackled and split apart. There was no energy, no juice left in me to scream. Then suddenly it stopped but my body, still reacting to the attack, did not relax.

"You see, I can make things quite unpleasant for you." The expression it wore was one of pity, but the gleam in its eyes was one of pure delight. While I remembered how to breathe it took a biscuit from the tea tray and spread a drop of jam across the top. I watched as the demon ate it slowly, delicately in three small bites.

I reached for the cup of tea and it smiled brightly at me. My hands felt like lumps at the end of my arms and my fingers wouldn't quite work the way they were supposed to. I ended up knocking the cup off the tray onto the floor. The demon clucked at me and picked the cup off the floor.

"We can get you another in just a moment. Unless that was a gesture on your part that you are willing to do this the civilized way?" I nodded, holding my tears in check. The thought of experiencing that limit of pain again made me cringe inside.

Obviously I was outclassed magically, hell, the demon had twice my powers. I had nothing to throw back but curses and dirty looks. I had to move this to a playing field where I had the advantage, or at least a chance. There was something it wanted from me, something that it couldn't get without me. If I'd at least tried to read the spell before running up the stairs after

Byron, I might have had something. If Agnes'
life wasn't in the balance, I probably would
have. My mind focused a bit when the demon
stood up.

"I'll get you another cup," it said graciously as
it moved out of the room.

Chapter 21

I tested my arms and legs. I could move them, but I felt clumsy and uncoordinated. I pushed myself off the couch and turned toward the window. Frozen, I surveyed bodies in various states of decay as they stood, looking through the window.

I stumbled back but they made no movement to enter the house. He did control them, or his magic did. I looked back toward the hallway and a white haired man was moving toward me. He was well dressed and had obviously taken care of himself in life. I couldn't see any blood stains or torn flesh on him, but his eyes had a haunted look with the dark circles under his eyes and the paleness of his cheeks.

I watched him, waiting to defend myself, but he stood where the hallway ended not quite making it to where I was standing by the couch. Even though there was no expression on his face, or rather, he only had one expression and it didn't change, I sensed a struggle. It reminded me of the old cartoons where the lady is tied up on the railroad track and she struggles to free herself.

I pushed out my will with a searching spell, curious to see what I'd find. It may have been that I wasn't sure what I was searching for, or maybe he was trying to meet me half way. A voice filled my head, an unfamiliar voice.

'In the other room, get the red book. Hurry.'

I paused for a moment, wondering if I should trust this voice. A warm sensation pulsed at my chest and I pulled out the locket with my sister's remains. I hope that was a sign that I could trust this.

I half walked and half stumbled into the other room. There was a bookshelf against the wall near the window where more zombies were just standing and swaying. I pulled the string to lower the blinds, and then turned to the bookshelf.

"You're not getting into trouble over there, are you?" I heard the demon call out. What were the chances that he could see through the zombie's eyes? I wasn't going to take any chances. Glancing over, the old man, zombie was staring at me. Shit.

The bookshelf was covered with books of all colors, but there… Wait a minute. This bookshelf wasn't here before, was it? I'd run in and out of here so fast I couldn't quite remember, but my gut feeling was that it hadn't been. I heard clacking from the kitchen and decided it didn't matter. There was only one red book on the shelf that was glowing like the podium and the magic circle in the rug. I pulled it out.

Conveniently, there was a bookmark in a page about projecting one's image. Hell this would have been useful a long time ago. I skimmed through the spell, trying to see what it required. I heard the floor creak as the old man shuffled over to me then looked at me with a sort of sternness I'd expect from a school principal.

The spell required a substitute, someone to hold the mass and presence of the person being projected. Not as cool as a hologram, but where was I going to find somebody. I looked up at the old man and shook my head. No way.

'Cast it. You don't have much time.' His thoughts broadcast into my head.

"You're a freaking zombie. What is this, some sort of trick?" I whispered furiously at the old man. He grunted and somehow I could feel him twisting inside his own body, trapped.

'Now, child. Now!' Somehow the emphasis hurt my head as though he were yelling into my ear.

I glanced around and began casting. The words seemed to take a life of their own as I whispered them, the normal push of magic didn't seem necessary. It was like I had asked if it might do this thing and the magic, as if impatient for me to ask already, was rushing out to meet me. It happened so fast I wondered if it had worked until I looked toward the old man and saw myself standing there.

My eyes were glassy, as if I was in shock. The old man, looking like me, shuffled into the other room toward the couch where I'd been sitting. It took my place, and waited for the demon to return. I looked down at myself and saw the wrinkled hands, the sweater vest, and felt the tightness of the leather shoes on my feet. This was so weird and so cool at the same time.

"Ah, there you are." The demon smiled as it returned to the living room. "Did you meet James? Nice chap, but a little bit of a wall flower, I'm afraid." It whispered the last part as if in confidence, even though I could hear them. Were all demons like this?

I moved slowly toward the podium, trying my best to look like a rambling zombie. I could feel their eyes on me from the other room but did my best to play my role. I could feel a braided cord of magic flowing between myself and James on the couch. I stopped and looked at myself sitting on that couch, not moving and just staring back at me.

How far did this spell go toward mimicking my actual self? Would I just sit there? Would I respond? Would that be up to the zombie playing me or would I have some control?

As my panic was growing a song started to play in my head. No, not a song. It was more like a child's rhyme. As my mind reached out to understand it, I realized that it was only sung like a child's rhyme. It was a spell of sorts. My eyes widened. Whispering the spell the faint sounds coming from my lips ended on the lips of my doppelganger.

"Never mind him, my dear. Let's talk about your future." I saw myself turn toward the demon and open its mouth.

"I thought we were going to talk about your sudden rise to power, Klemnoth." The demon looked sharply toward my doppelganger. I have to say I was a bit surprised. I'd meant to give him some safe answer that would not invoke additional pain. Could I even feel it from here?

"I see your boyfriend has told you more than you let on. Good, good." Even from here I could see the subtle changes rippling through its form. "It is so much better for us to be honest. To be on the same level."

'Stop wasting time, child. Get to the spell. I can only distract it for so long.' The voice in my head urged.

I quietly shuffled over to the podium while trying to tune out the conversation going on across the room. The podium was located on the edge of the circle. I placed my hands on it, just to see if it was real. It felt like polished wood. The spell lay on top and perfectly readable in its complexity. The circle must keep the demon from finding it and the podium somehow, well, it was vibrating with power. It must somehow help focus and balance the spell.

The demon needed someone to pull the spell from the podium and out of the circle. But why all the theatrics?

If I could get a protection spell up while I was casting it might give me a second chance if my first attempt failed. I checked to see how the conversation was going in the other room. No one looked up at me as they were embroiled in verbal fisticuffs.

"You had to steal another's power to earn your glory. It's a disgrace. You poor, weak, pitiful thing." I heard my voice ring out across the rooms. It was followed by a menacing snarl. Oh shit.

I pulled my will and focused it on casting my defenses. The protection spell began, but this time it started on the edges of the circle, as if it were a natural fit. I layered it stronger than I ever had before until it felt like it was three feet thick. Wanting to throw on some avoidance to the outer edges but seeing things escalating in the other room I decided to get started.

The spell was more complex than I'd ever seen before. My eyes rolled down the sheet and the pit of my stomach grew cold. This was way above my abilities. This thing was so complex that... What if something happened? What if I made a mistake and made things irreparably worse? My heart was racing and then I looked up into the living room.

The fine clothes ripped away at the demon's back and the skin melted from its form. The smell of brimstone and ash filled the room in a puff of smoke. Its laugh was deep and resonating and I could feel my arms and legs turning to rubber once again. All the fear, all the doubts. I was the wrong person for this. The world needed someone stronger, someone who could do this thing. I looked back at the spell and a single tear fell down my cheek to the floor.

The ring grew brighter, an almost bluish white. It rose up in a column around me, on the edges of the magic circle. The columns were like fun house mirrors, only at all angles around me and none of them had my reflection. Instead my sister stood looking at me. Her eyes watching as they always had when we were kids and I was about to show her a spell I'd completed.

I reached out to touch her and felt a sharp stinging sensation. The walls dropped, but my finger was left swelling with blood. It fell to the floor and the power hummed in my head and through me, vibrating without moving at all. I looked up and saw the astonished looks on the old man's face, and the leering demon that stood across the coffee table from him. The projection spell had been broken with whatever was happening now.

Everything seemed to have been ripped from me, all the past, present and future. I wasn't in the real world anymore. I was higher than that, looking in at the world. I adjusted the spell on the podium and I began to read.

The words felt strange in my mouth, as I spoke them, rolling along my tongue and resonating through my throat and lips. Yet it rolled, almost automatically.

I could see the demon charging the circle, its frightful appearance tearing at my defenses. But I couldn't feel the fear, the anger, the sadness, the joy or pride or any of it. I just kept reading.

Chapter 22

Even as layer upon layer of my protection spell
fell to the blows of this thing I kept speaking.
Every time it ripped a hole in one side, the rest
of the layers shifted to protect the opening. It
was strange, as if it were alive and conscious
that it had a job to do and it was willing to
sacrifice parts of itself to allow me to finish.

"Listen to me, human wizard child. And hear
me well." Its voice was now a serious of hisses
and growled words. "The only way you can
save your sister is to take my deal."

I paused, almost finished, the protection spell
almost gone. The demon took advantage of the
moment to continue.

"While that spell may remove the infection it
will not bring back the dead." He laughed at my
expression and I winced at the sound. "The
dead, the true dead and the infected that have
met their final ends, they will stay in the
afterlife. They are my trophies, of which you
have sent me many."

Instinctively I reached up to hold the locket
which was now cold. Was I giving up my only
chance to save her, to bring her back? Or was
he lying to serve his own purposes? I didn't
know whether the spell would do any of what

he said; all I knew is that it was supposed to fix everything.

I felt another blow to the protective circle and I knew that it wouldn't last much longer. It was either finish the spell now or take the demon's deal. I thought of my sister, of JD, of my parents, of Byron and Agnes and all the others. Could I let the world down for just one person?

I continued the spell, I couldn't take the chance on being tricked.

"Will you be able to forgive yourself, child wizard, if you do not even attempt to save her? Who is to blame if not for you?" I stopped reciting and looked at him, fury blazing in my eyes. "Yes, hatred and fear, they are like milk and cookies to me. But it is in my nature to do these things. I have given you the choice, the option to try again. How can you blame anyone but yourself?"

He stepped back as if to concede. I took a breath to sigh and saw him charge the protective circle. The barrier broke and he flew into the circle.

An unearthly scream resounded in my ears as I used my last breath to speak the last syllable and the magic poured forth out of me and spread encompassing warmth around the circle and up through the roof and into the sky. I could feel it as it exploded through me into the world, this warmth. In my mind and down to my very soul I spread this warmth and I could feel it all.

The magic swirled around me and I felt lifted off the ground, lifted into a place where there are no words to describe it. Every fiber of my being was a conduit for the magic I was sending into the world. There's no way to explain but it felt like my life, my love, my strength, all of it was taken from me, multiplied and dished out into the world and at the same time returned to me with interest. Every thought ceased to exist and for a moment I may have reached the Zen state of nothingness.

There really is a journey to and from that place, but I don't know that I'll get there again in this lifetime. There is quietness of the mind, the soul and of the world. Nothing I could even come close to understanding, not that I'd try. I remember going through the motions, looking around the room at the chaos there.

I'm not really sure what happened after that. Everything went chaotic and felt right and wrong at the same time. When I became aware again I realized that Klemnoth wasn't there, thank goodness for small favors. I guess I prefer to think of that thing being burned with the magic and the light that happened that day. I vaguely remember sizzling or maybe it was the steam and I imagined the sizzling. Either way the room was clear when I woke up.

James was standing outside the circle, whispering to me. He'd lost that blank stare and looked healthy and human again. He couldn't seem to cross the boundary of the circle for some reason without my permission. I couldn't think of a reason why not so I let him. He helped me up and half carried me upstairs to a guest bedroom.

We found Byron curled up in a corner; Agnes' body was gone somehow. I didn't have the energy to worry about it. Apparently the demon hadn't seen fit to take him out of the state where he relived his family's death over and over again. James eased me onto the floor to help the man.

Byron had almost successfully removed his eyes with his fingernails. The blood dribbled down his face onto his clothes and the floor. James kept trying to talk with him, soothe him. I watched with apathy at the scene and fell asleep on the floor there until James helped me up and into a guest bedroom to sleep.

James was able to subdue Byron long enough for the hospital to pick him up. They found all kinds of drugs in his system but for the most part he was a vegetable with suicidal tendencies. They were able to keep him alive by feeding him on an IV and pumping drugs into his system to keep him calm. Last I heard, he successfully took his own life about three months later.

In my dreams I vaguely remember pieces of what happened as I was being ushered downstairs by James. The feeling like I was missing someone, that I'd forgotten something. I remember telling James what had happened, but it seemed like he already knew. He held me up at one point too, I think. It was like he was searching my eyes for something, but I was too exhausted to care. I couldn't remember why it was important until later. He was doing the same check I'd had years ago when they'd denied me wizard training.

As my head hit the pillow, I found myself crying and darkness enveloped me again.

The world was still a mess and would be for a while. The spell did its job to restore the infected people to their former selves including a neat feature where limbs that were lost during the time suddenly weren't lost anymore. That would have been awkward and left a lot of job openings.

Most people had no memory of what happened. In fact, the three months when the world had been filled with zombies seemed to have been replaced with mundane memories of life as we know it. I found myself a little jealous and bitter about that.

Those survivors that held out to the end had their memories erased just like the infected. Apparently the amnesia only affected non-magical folks. The rest were under the impression that something bad had happened but they weren't sure what and no one wanted to talk about it. They mourned the loss of the ones that died, but it was somehow muted. Like a news story about something that happened around the world to someone else.

Those that had died by their own hand or killed while under the influence of the infection were still dead. I still felt ambiguous about that one. I mean, if I'd known there was another way to save them or if my life hadn't been in constant danger or if I was killing them for fun, maybe I'd feel worse. I couldn't help the situation or my lack of knowledge of the coming solution to the entire world's zombie problem. The only thing that still chaffed was keeping myself from thinking about the demon's offer to do it all over again. The things that might have been done differently. Damn the demon.

Still the dead, they had already been taken to a better place, right? And, since there weren't riots or mass rage at the loss, I decided that I ought to let it go too.

Apparently some part of the spell repaired physical things as well. The rubble, the broken down cars, the looting and break-ins never happened. It was like a big reset button had been pressed. Even with the thousands of thousands dead, the world was content to move on with a sad shrug. The only people left wondering were those who remembered what had happened. I know I couldn't explain it.

246

"You can stay here," offered James. "We need to have a meeting of the Elders and the Council will need to discuss this. It will be imperative for you to attend. We'll need to decide what to do with you anyway."

I gave him a hard look, which he met with a neutral one. He was letting me know that I'd been ousted from the magical community and the consequences were sure to follow me. In fact he'd been helpful and supportive since I'd woken, even went into town and bought a messenger bag and a change of clothes for me. I grabbed the bag now and threw it over my shoulder.

"You want me. Come and find me." I told him. He chuckled and motioned toward the bag. I felt into the front pocket and pulled out a plane ticket home.

He looked at me, and I got the impression that there was more kindness there than I'd believed any of the Elders could possess. I turned and jetted out the front door. He'd already called a cab and it was parked waiting for me in front of the house. I found out when I got to the airport, he'd already paid the cabbie too.

Chapter 23

As anxious as I was to get home, I dreaded it too. I went back to our apartment, the one I'd shared with Sophia. The summoning circle was still exposed, sitting there like an unspoken accusation.

Everything was as I'd left it, from the books to all the things we'd collected together over the years. All of them were memories of better times and all of it reminders that I'd sacrificed a chance to save her to restore the world. Perfect strangers across the world and I'd sacrificed the one person I cared about the most. Yes, I'd killed her, I'd taken her life and even when those around us had come back none of them were her.

It took me a couple of weeks to pack everything into a U-Haul. I had to spend a little extra time deconstructing the summoning circle. Once I was done I dropped off the next month's rent to the landlord and let her know that the apartment was free effective immediately. She was politely concerned about the late notice, but didn't put up too much of a fight considering all our deposits and the pre-paid last month's rent would go directly into her pocket.

I'm sure my experiences have influenced me, but I enjoyed the West Coast, so I drove in that direction hoping to make plans as opportunities came up. I couldn't bear living with the memories of what had happened, with what I'd done to Sophia there. The town, the neighborhood, all of it seemed tainted. The confusion of where to lay the blame was harder to bear. The demon had been right about that bit, at least, damn its hide.

I took my time driving across the country, stopping at camp grounds, doing a little sightseeing. I still woke up screaming from the nightmares, but I'd learned to muffle it with a pillow. The nightmares didn't seem to be getting any less frequent and I had no one to turn to for help. Any psychiatrist worth his education would have me committed for talking about the walking dead in any realistic way.

Travel was easier and almost comforting. I sometimes found myself speeding up to find a town where I could stay before the sun touched down before remembering that things were different now. The instinct was still there, the raw need to survive still pulsed in the back of my brain.

I got to meet people along the way. It was still a novelty at times to see a person or a group of people looking out at the same scene. I wanted to hug them and tell them how glad I was that they were in this world and not walking corpses, rotting to the bone. I contained my crazy, but I found myself smiling at people more. I was more appreciative for every new face I saw. And more than that, I appreciated the ordered chaos that their presence brought to the world.

When I reached California, I found a cheap hotel near a mall and explored the depths of my girlish nature. I got my hair cut and highlights put in, my nails became an orangish-red and as it was a special savings deal, I got my first pedicure. There weren't a lot of options, but I found an outfit that was a bit outside my budget range, but looked spectacular on me. I was ready to settle down.

The next morning I headed straight for the Bay Area and JD's summer house. The low laying branches scraped the top of the U-Haul, but I was more concerned with the damage to the trees than the truck. The driveway was clear and I parked where I thought I would be more visible. No one answered the door.

I suppose I shouldn't have been as disappointed as I was, but I had hoped that we would have the sort of reunion I'd been fantasizing about for the past month. I reasoned as I drove back through the tree covered lane, that he might not want a reminder of all that had happened. That hurt, but I couldn't blame him. Knowing that he'd caused the world such hardship and loss, he'd probably want to forget more than I did. Then again, maybe he'd lost his memories along with all the people who were non-magical.

The Bay Area, San Francisco in particular, while packed with people was also a bit nerve wracking after a few days. Post-traumatic stress disorder, I think they call it. I'd hear movement in the hotel hallway and suddenly be on my guard looking for my weapons before I'd realize that everything was back to normal. I'd settle down again and be on full alert at the next sound. I was becoming too jittery and cancelled my appointments for apartment tours. Besides, I'd gotten this feeling that I was being watched and it made me itch.

I took some time to look through websites, looking for small towns and quiet areas. I still wanted to be around people, I just didn't want to jump every time there was a sound nearby, especially at night. It looked like Canada was a bit more appealing, but the immigration laws might be a tad difficult. Still, even if I didn't make it there, I could find a place in one of the little towns along the Washington border. So I began my journey north once again.

Traffic on I5 was much different this time. You know how everyone hates traffic? I never really expected to love traffic, but the flow of vehicles was amazingly convenient. If you need some perspective, get out of your car and push it about three to five feet. Then do that thirty or forty times over and over every few miles. I'm sure I'll get tired of traffic someday.

Around Salem I got a call from Sunshine, the Reaper. Don't know how she got my cell number, but I could've had a heart attack when its tone went off in the seat beside me. She apologized and quickly filled me in on her adventure after she'd disappeared that fateful day.

It seemed that Klemnoth was aware of her limitation to teleport, or whatever, as such a new Reaper. Apparently she'd been pretty pissed to find out she'd been buried alive, well, as alive as a Reaper can be anyway. She'd miscalculated which direction she needed to go and dug a few feet in the wrong direction before figuring it out. I gave the appropriate sounds of oohs and ahhs, but continued to drive as she relayed the horrors of ruining her manicure. He'd had a bit of a sense of humor because he'd stuck her somewhere out in a field in the middle of France.

Eventually she got around to the second topic that she wanted to discuss with me. She was looking to get into a rental situation and offered me a place to stay. I didn't ask her how she knew I was moving, but I couldn't see the harm in accepting an offer to sleep on her couch.

"Casey, it'll be your couch, so don't worry about it."

"What do you mean?" I asked a bit distracted as I changed lanes to make my way around a slow moving semi.

"I need a roommate and since you're looking to move anyway, I figured, perfect setup." There was a pause on the line. "Look, before you say 'no', hear me out, ok?" The line went static for a moment then cleared. "The only way I can get out on my own is to be able to, you know, support a place to live. I wouldn't do well on the streets, I'm too cute."

"Where are you staying now." I asked as I changed lanes. She grumbled in response before answering.

"They have this halfway house for newbies, which I'm totally not anymore. Some of the older ones can get away with murder. Not literally of course, but still. They get all the perks and I have to find my own way in the world. I can't stay here any longer. My roommate is a pig." She paused to take a breath, but before I could say anything she continued. "Anyway, since you're looking for a place and I found the perfect three bedroom condo, I figured we could, you know, help each other out."

"Ummm."

"Oh please Casey! Please do this for me." I found myself smiling in spite of it all.

"Sure. If it's still available by the time I get up there—"

"We're already on the lease. Just one of my many perks that we can all benefit from. Ok, I'll see you when you get here."

She hung up before I could ask for the address. Hitting redial on the phone showed that no calls had been received. There was nothing to do but laugh and drive on. It would all work itself out.

When I arrived in Portland an hour or so later, I made a point to avoid going near the Willaker house. I wasn't sure how that situation was going to work out and I didn't want to owe him any more favors. Things were bad enough with the Council knowing about me, but fraternizing with the enemy wasn't a good idea for either of us probably.

Sunshine had got in touch with me a few minutes after I hit Portland. Her directions were a little hard to understand, but I finally made it to the townhouse she'd been talking about. Yeah, a freaking townhouse. It was definitely a step up from an apartment, I would find out.

We had a little talk about finances and the like. She was evasive on how my signature got on the lease agreement and the roommate situation. And I didn't mention that the Council was likely to be gunning for me in the near future. We did a little budget crunching though. I found out that she had stored up a small cash pile from sources I just didn't want to know about anyway and she learned that with the remaining savings I had in the bank, we could afford the place for about three months. That would give us time to find legitimate jobs and get on track. Somehow it was just agreed that we'd try to make it work.

Our new home was actually pretty nice. The walls weren't connected to the neighbors on either side and seemed to be built with sound insulation in mind. There was a postage sized lawn out back with a poorly maintained flowerbed skirting the edges of the lawn and fence. The sliding glass door even opened on to a cement pad that seemed more like a stoop than a deck. Sunshine had put a couple of cheap, white plastic chairs out there for sitting outside enjoying the sounds of the neighborhood. There was even enough room and privacy to layout a protection spell for late night spell practice.

The front had no yard except for the small rectangles of bushes and intermittent trees on the other side of the sidewalk from the house. There was a garage door at the lowest level, almost the basement, and wide and tall steps leading to the main floor. There was a wrought iron handrail on either side of the steps and every other step contained a large pot with soil topped with bits of moss and dead leaves. Finally in front of the steps was a largish deciduous tree blocking, in part, the view of anyone coming or going into the place. It was really kind of perfect.

A couple of guys from across the street helped get the furniture up the stairs and into place. They seemed eager enough, but I'm pretty sure it had something to do with my new roommate flirting with them. If it kept me from having to haul the couches and beds up those stairs, so be it.

When everything was in its proper room and all things of immediate need had been unboxed, I ordered a celebration first pizza for our new home and invited the guys to join us. After a quick shower, and apparently a beer run, the guys returned with a couple of six packs and certain expectations. We kicked them out around ten, unsatisfied, of course, and went to sleep in our new home.

Sunshine didn't have any furniture so I let her have Sophia's old bed. I gave her fair warning that it was used and by whom, but it didn't seem to bother her. She was just happy to get away from the halfway house and her pig of a roommate there. I was glad to have one less piece of furniture to store or throw away.

Chapter 24

It was nice to worry about mundane things following the spontaneous rental and move-in. My first order of business was to get a job, meet new people and figure out what I was going to do. There was a bit of a culture disconnect from my old lifestyle, but I didn't feel like I needed to hurry. Well, not much anyway.

A few days later I was sitting in the living room frowning over my resume when the doorbell rang. I shuffled through the living room and opened the door to find JD standing there, flowers in hand and that same boyish smile on his face as he gave me a once over.

"Looks like we need to go shopping again."

The shock of the situation, of seeing him when I'd already written him off and the reference to our time together short circuited my brain. I shut the door in his face and went back into the living room. Sunshine tsk'd me as she opened the door and invited crazy pants back into my life.

He sat down next to me on the couch and offered the flowers. When I didn't take them he sigh, placed them on the coffee table and took my hands in his.

"I guess I have some explaining to do." Only then did I look at his eyes and the face I'd both fantasized about and woken in a cold sweat when nightmares wouldn't let me save him. I wanted so much to hold him, but the fear that he'd be taken away from me again made me timid.

"I thought you were--" My voice cracked and we both sat there for a moment in silence.

"The barrier spell you cast on me was a little tough to get out of with the owners gone. If a concerned neighbor hadn't come by I might still be there." He touched the side of my face, gently. "I was always coming to find you again. You know that don't you."

He leaned in and I pulled back a bit. He stopped, uncertain whether he should try again. My eyes filled with tears.

"You can't just keep doing this to me."

"Doing what?" He reached up and gently tucked a lock of hair behind my ear. "Saving you?"

"Yes."

In a moment I was swept into his arms and lifted onto his lap with his lips claiming mine. The world melted away and time stopped. Our caresses, our heat was building to epic proportions.

"Ew, guys," said a disgusted Sunshine. "Get a room. Preferably one you're paying rent on."

I grabbed a decorative pillow and chucked it at her.

In short, Sunshine and JD had had a meeting of the minds. There was some sort of truce, shaky as it was, and an agreement that some financial assistance would be necessary. Somehow Sunshine had convinced JD to rent the last bedroom, paying a year in advance. It worked out for everyone. JD had an excuse to come over whenever he wanted, Sunshine and I had an extension on our timeframe for finding jobs in a tough job market and JD and I had some time to get to know each other in a more casual setting.

It was nice to be able to talk to someone about the nightmares and about the feeling that I was still trapped in a desolate world. He'd had similar feelings and reactions, although he didn't admit to waking up in the night screaming like a little girl. He did offer to comfort me in my bed no matter the hour or the state of undress.

He told me that he only vaguely remembered what it had been like to be a zombie. The haunted look in his eyes told a different story. He muttered something about never-ending hunger and a wild chaos and somehow I just understood. He also confessed that his powers were returned to him, but I got the sense that he was afraid to use them or that there was some consequence he wasn't telling me. I didn't pry. He would tell me in his own time.

We settled into some normalcy, the three of us. Once a week we have a movie night.

Sometimes we invite the neighbors over, other times not. We watch just about everything, but one theme of movie is prohibited. It's an unspoken agreement that is respected by all of us. No zombie movies.

Turn the page for an exciting preview of
Cynthia Gilstrap's next Casey Jones novel.

Council's Nightmare

Coming May 2013!

Chapter One

"Tell me your greatest weakness and how you've overcome it," asked the plump woman sitting across from me as she glanced at my resume for the fortieth time in the twenty minutes we'd been talking. She looked up from the paper and smiled at me.

I hated these questions. I'd been answering them for the past six months until I wanted to scream and there never seemed to be an end to them. In fact, I'd been told on more than one occasion that I would be perfect for the job, only to get an email or letter in the mail a few days later that the position had been filled by someone more qualified. It was enough to make one cynical about the whole thing.

I smiled, gave my response, got the polite chuckle and the interview moved on. My mind wandered a bit as the familiar song and dance continued. I'd been asked the same questions so many times my answers were smooth, inflections, body language, smile and all.

Almost nine months ago I wouldn't have had to answer these sorts of questions. Of course, there'd been other problems. Top among those was finding food, bullets and shelter on a daily basis. At that time, most of the world had been infected with a magically-altered virus that left the denizens with gaping wounds, a lowered IQ and the need to eat any living soul slow enough to be caught.

I'd found the source, a demon by the name of Klemnoth, who'd stolen the powers of a sorcerer and inflicted hell on earth. It had taken the mother of all spells to set the world right again but it didn't stop my nightmares. For most people, non-magical folks mostly, that meant having their memories wiped of the zombie pandemic and the resulting destruction. It also had the effect of smoothing over the memories of those killed or lost in the battles while they were zombies. Still, you'd think there would be some reward for saving the world, right?

The woman on the other side of the desk cleared her throat. I looked up, startled, and realized that she'd asked me a question and I hadn't been paying attention.

"I'm sorry," I said as I adjusted myself in the plastic chair she'd offered me. "Could you explain what you mean?"

She smiled politely and asked the question again, with examples of how one might respond. I smiled back as brightly as I could and answered another one of those, what-would-you-do type of question. All of them the same and none of them seemed to amount to much. Still, I had to try. I needed to pay rent.

JD, my boyfriend and aforementioned sorcerer who'd had his powers stolen, had been living off and on again with me and my roommate, Sunshine. Even though he dropped by when he wanted to and didn't really stay with us all the time, he'd had the decency to pay for a year in advance. JD came from a wealthy family and with his share of the rent Sunshine and I had put it into a joint savings account and used the money to pay our landlord while we looked for and found jobs. Well, Sunshine had found a job. She served as a bartender in a bar a few blocks from home within three weeks of looking, but I'd found nothing but apologetic thank you letters.

"Well, those are all the questions I have for you." She tapped my resume on the desk and looked up at me expectantly. "Is there anything you would like to know about the company or the position?"

"Thank you, Judith, no." I stood up, patted the wrinkles from my skirt and reached my hand to shake hers. It was time to finish this dance.

"Well, I do appreciate you coming down here to speak with me. I can assure you that you seem to be a very good candidate for the position, but I will tell you that there are two other candidates in line for the position so don't get too excited." She leaned in conspiratorially and whispered, "I think you may have the job, young lady, but don't hold me to that. Anything could happen."

Yeah, anything.

I thanked Judith, trying to appear confident and interested. It's hard to control your cynicism when you've heard the same thing time and time again with no results. Worse is when you get that rejection letter and you don't have the money to run out for a drink or a tub of ice cream.

Once outside, I pulled my sunglasses from my purse and looked up to the blue skies above. There may be sunshine and blue right now, but the nip in the air hinted at rain tonight. It seemed that the cold and rain that everyone complained about in Portland was about to begin.

My heels clicked down the sidewalk, dodging other pedestrians and cracks in the sidewalk, as I made my way toward the commuter train that ran through the city. It was inexpensive, fast and mostly reliable. Plus, it was all I had.

I was about a block away when I felt eyes on the back of my head. Glancing around casually, I pretended to be unsure whether I was on the correct block to see if I could spot anyone paying undue attention to me. There didn't seem to be anyone, but that didn't mean there wasn't someone there, so I took quick stock of the faces and moved toward the train platform.

When I reached the corner, I turned and leaned against the building. As I waited, I considered pulling up a protection spell, but if my attendant was from the Council that could get me in even more hot water with them. The Council wasn't too pleased about the spell I'd cast to save the world, even if it had saved them in the process. They were kind of picky about who could and could not do magic, regardless of the circumstances, and I was unsure whether they were authorized to kill me if they found me casting magic here and now.

The Council is a collection of wizards cultivated from families who have tracked generations of magic users through the ages. I'm sure if you asked any of them, they could draw a family tree back to Merlin. You know they all go back to Merlin. I couldn't tell you how I fit into that family tree though, since I was evaluated and denied magical training when I was a kid. I guess I was one of those outliers.

Training from a young age is necessary to develop the full potential of a wizard. The Council keeps track, as best they can anyway, of families and family names that have been recorded to have any potential abilities. When a child is of age to be tested, whether the parents are aware of it or not, they are taken to some place with dark hallways and eerie questions. Somehow they determine how much magical ability is present and then based on criteria that I'd never had explained to me, they decided whether the child should be given a mentor and trained in the arts.

I like to think that if there was a bloodline, shared by all the families with wizarding abilities, that there were a few unexpected children created out of wedlock or whatnot and they pop up now and again. I'm not sure if that is the case, mind you, but it seems like the magical ability is hereditary. It makes sense that if you were trying to corner the market on those abilities you would do well to find the strongest ones, make them loyal to you and control their actions.

Maybe I'm just bitter. They chose not to train me. It was only a child's curiosity that I found out what they were testing me for and what I might be able to become. There had been another child being tested at the same time, a rather pompous, overindulged brat named Marcus. I hadn't known the words to describe him at the time, but I still remembered the conversation.

He'd enjoyed showing how knowledgeable he was about the process and the reasons for testing. He'd laughed as he'd told me that my blood was probably too diluted to make it into full use of my powers and how he had come from a long line of pure blooded wizards. He taunted me until I was close to tears, and when he thought I was close to the edge he told me that his family had been working on clearing out the impurities like me from the wizarding world.

I'd planned on hitting him, but at that moment a stern looking woman had come to take Marcus for testing. He smirked at me as he walked through that door and I'll never forget the surge of anger and determination I felt in that moment. I was going to be the best wizard ever.

I waited until they'd shut the door behind them, before I made my move. I grabbed my bag and took an unguided tour of the facilities. It was by some luck in my journey that I didn't run into anyone. It was also my good fortune to enter an elaborate classroom which gave me a glimpse into what I could expect if I passed their magic tests.

There was a desk at the front, a large wooden desk with an adult sized chair and blackboards covering the wall behind it. There were about a dozen student desks, all completely clean and orderly. On the remaining three walls were bookshelves with a space on each wall for floor-to-ceiling bookshelves. I was enamored and more determined than ever to pass their tests.

I guess I got it into my head that I had to know magic to pass the test. This room seemed a perfect place to get a few zingers to show them. I scanned the books, but they didn't really make sense to me. I'd stuffed my bag full by the time I got concerned that they would find me missing. I had a very random selection of books as I found out later.

Having collected something to give me an edge, I returned to the waiting room. Before I could crack open my bag to pull out one of the books, however, I was called in to be tested. For years I've tried to remember what they did exactly, but everything associated with that test is a blank in my mind. I'm not sure if it was a spell of some kind or just that I was young. I'm not even sure how I got home. If it hadn't been for the bag full of books on basic magic use I might have forgotten being tested at all.

I sighed. Those memories combined with the sun shining down, were making me sleepy and I almost forgot that I was being followed. I suspected that this was just some patrol to keep an eye on me while the Council decided what to do, but I liked knowing who was tailing me in case it came in handy later. There's no better way to get around someone than if they are unaware that you know who they are.

I counted the faces coming down the block, checked them against the ones I'd counted in my look around before and waited for the quick turn of the head to evade detection. So far, all of them seemed to be interested in getting across the street to the train platform. Then, I saw him.

He was about five and a half tall, dark-brown hair, sunglasses and a business suit with elaborate cuff links that gleamed in the sun. The slight glance in my direction, a very brief and almost unremarkable pause, and then he continued across the street. Gotcha!

I pushed myself off the wall and walked across the street to the train stop. There was a section of today's paper on the end of one of the benches and I picked it up to read it while waiting for the train. It didn't occur to me that I'd walked into their trap until I felt the spell close around me, cutting off sound and light.

I stood, frozen in darkness, waiting for something to happen. This was new, I thought. I was pretty sure I wasn't dead because I could feel my heart pounding in my chest painfully and it wasn't a nightmare because the people I'd accompanied to the train weren't blood and gore crusted zombies, as all my nightmares do.

A point of light appeared in the the blackness. It seemed to grow as I watched and expanded until I was back in the sun again. Before me now stood a scrawny delivery boy; he perched on ten-speed bike, his blonde hair tousled and windswept. The only indication that he worked for the Council was the faint trace of his family mark on his forehead which would be visible only to those who could see magic.

"Delivery. Official business." I took stock of him as he pulled a wax sealed envelope from his delivery bag in a smooth, elegant motion. He was as tall as I was, way too skinny, but he his arms and legs looked corded with muscle. "Casey Danvers, you are called to appear on the eve of the next full moon."

"English, please." He pushed the envelope toward me but I stood without moving. He sighed.

"Three days from now. Instructions are here." I took the envelope and before I could look up to thank him he had gone. I don't mean travelled on his bike up the street, he was just not there anymore.

I felt the seal under my thumb. Rumors of people getting these, but I'd never held one in my hand before. Once they'd dropped me back home after the test, the Council had never had reason to know me or suspect that I was one of the more active rebel wizards acting in the world.

There isn't a group or anything. Word gets out that there is a wizard not playing by the Council rules and they quickly becomes a memory. The

Council is quick to end insubordination and rebellion.

My legs were a little wobbly when I got on the train. I'd found a seat and plopped myself down, never taking my eyes from the envelope I couldn't bring myself to open. I knew they'd be getting in contact with me. I'd done a lot of casting and shown too much ability for someone who'd never been trained in the magical arts. They had to know. I just didn't know what they were going to do or why they hadn't done it by now.

A man sitting next to me tapped me on the shoulder. He was an older gentleman, dressed casually and he had kind eyes. He pointed at my bag, which I now realized was vibrating and ringing. I smiled in thanks and dug my cell phone out.

"This is Casey."

"Babe," JD's voice purred over the line. "I know its date night, but something came up."

"Must be pretty important," I growled. "This is the third one you've missed. In a row, I might add. Most girlfriends like to have a bit more attention than once a month."

He chuckled. There seemed to be voices and what sounded like an intercom announcement.

"You'll live." He turned to talk with someone, but over the noise of the train and the kids a few seats up I couldn't make out any details.

"Are you at the airport?" I heard the phone being shuffled around.

"Hold on a second." He said something I couldn't quite make out and then returned. "Yeah, I've got to take care of some family business. You know the drill."

"I thought you just got done working on family business." I could feel myself starting to whine. I wanted to be pampered, to share this albatross of a summons with someone and have that someone wrap his arms around me and tell me that everything would be all right. "How long will you be gone this time?"

"Hopefully not long." The phone was shifted again. "Maybe a week. It could be less than that. I'm not sure."

"Is it something you could, you know, postpone?"

"What's wrong?" His voice got hard and serious and I knew that he was probably standing in the airport, oblivious to the traffic moving around him. "What happened?"

"I, uh," Suddenly I had an attack of indecision. Should I tell him about the letter and make him worry? I didn't even know what the summons was about. It could be something trivial and I'd be worrying him for nothing. On the other hand, I could be summoned to be executed and we'd never see each other again.

"I miss you is all. We've hardly gotten to see each other since you've been doing all this extra work for your dad."

"I love you too, Casey. It won't be long." He hung up. JD didn't like goodbyes since the last time we'd been forced to say it.

Guilt and fear mixed around in my stomach the entire ride home. I told myself that if it were bad I could just call him up and he'd return home. Part of me argued that there wasn't much he could do about Council decisions anyway and why should he be tortured alongside me with the waiting and not knowing. Still, some part of me knew that I was wrong.

An avid reader of paranormal stories, watcher
of zombie movies, and a twisted romantic at
heart, Cynthia Gilstrap is a freelance wrtier and
day-dreamer who lives in Portland, Oregon.
This is her first novel.